FATHER'S DAY . . .

Syd Bishop spoke, his voice gruff. "Nothing could have happened to her, could it?" "That's what we're going to find out," said the Toff.

Syd flung himself out of the house, slamming the door so hard that the walls seemed to shake. The Toff turned away and went upstairs. He wanted to talk to Pop—obviously the boy was frightened as well as resentful of his father. Ten minutes with the older man might prove valuable.

Rollison pushed the bedroom door open. A man was lying on the bed, his eyes staring toward the ceiling. He seemed strangely still. Then the Toff saw the single gash across his throat.

The awful thing was that, apart from a dark-red patch on the pillow on either side of his neck, there was no sign of blood . . .

A BUNDLE
FOR THE TOFF

John Creasey

PRESTIGE BOOKS • NEW YORK

A BUNDLE FOR THE TOFF

PRESTIGE BOOKS INC. • 18 EAST 41ST STREET
NEW YORK, N.Y. 10017

CONTENTS

1

BUNDLE ON THE THRESHOLD

The heart of London is large, to some it is warm, to others, perhaps to very many others, it is as cold as ice. In that heart live human beings of all classes and of all income groups, from duke to dustman, from millionaire to pauper.

Perhaps one of the most remarkable is the Honorable Richard Rollison, known for many excellent reasons as "the Toff." Good-looking, rich and adventurous, he mixes freely with both the social élite and the underworld. It has been said that no one ever turned to him for help in vain. According to his man Jolly he is overgenerous; certainly he has been known to open his pocket and his home to ex-convicts to whom few others would give house-room.

One bitter cold night in March, the Toff had been dining a little more freely than usual. It was many years since he had drunk sufficiently to loosen his tongue, but occasionally the right food, the right wine and the right companion, put an added sparkle in his eyes.

This was such a night.

The elderly taxi-driver who watched him unlock the street door of the house in Gresham Terrace where he had his flat knew him quite well. He did not know the lady with him, but the street lamp shone down on her, revealing the unquestionable fact that she was beautiful.

The door opened, and Rollison and his companion went inside.

It was only a little after twelve o'clock, so the night could still, by the sophisticated, be considered young. It was therefore quite conceivable that the Honorable Richard was going to change his shoes or his shirt or

7

even his deep purple cummerbund, before going on to dance at a night club, or take his chance at a casino. It was equally conceivable that Perdita Shortt was going simply to conduct some running repairs to stocking or bra. There was no reason at all why, as they reached the first of three landings on the dimly lit, unromantic stone staircase, they should not pause, and without a word, embrace.

After all, Richard Rollison was in his forties, and a bachelor. And Perdita Shortt was a widow in her thirties, a widow, moreover, excessively endowed with the world's, as well as a woman's, goods.

A stranger, regarding the couple dispassionately, would almost certainly have approved of the obvious pleasure each took in the other's company. He might well have followed their progress up the stairs with benign indulgence, noting Rollison's arm about Perdita's waist. The light, such as it was, seemed to make their eyes glow even more brightly—eyes already bright with the sparkle of champagne.

At the next landing, they dallied a little longer.

"Perdita," whispered the Toff.

"Yes," whispered Perdita.

"You are a very, very, beautiful woman."

"You are a very, very, handsome man."

"So long as you realize that I am a man."

"Are you beginning to wonder whether I'm a woman?" asked Perdita. She held her head back and looked at him through half-closed lashes.

"I think I know," Rollison said. "But I'm very hard to convince about anything."

"I'll convince you," Perdita promised, and her laughter carried a challenge which Rollison was unable to ignore.

It was one of the very few occasions when he forgot the dangers inherent in such a situation, for once inside his flat, they would be alone. Jolly, his man, was away visiting a sick brother, and there were those who said that, but for Jolly, the Toff would have been married at least a dozen times over.

Perdita and Rollison went slowly up the next flight of stairs and started, even more slowly, arms linked, up the next and last.

Reaching the landing and the stout, chestnut-colored door of Number 22g, they noticed nothing untoward. Rollison, in his temporary enchantment, had forgotten, and Perdita had never realized, that anything from poison gas to a bullet, from a prize-fighter to a pick-pocket, or from a murderer to a policeman, might be waiting in grim or deadly welcome.

Rollison took out his key ring, inserted the key unerringly into the lock while still looking at Perdita, and pushed the door.

"My home," he announced. "My castle."

"My lord," Perdita said, "I am a paralytic."

"You are a *what?*"

"A paralytic. When about to enter strange castles, the muscles of my legs become atrophied, and I cannot walk."

"Ah," said Rollison, sensing danger, unable, nevertheless, to resist playing with it. "You mean you feel as timid as a bride, and must be carried over the threshold?"

"You are most discerning," Perdita murmured. "Of course, if you're not man enough to carry me——"

She laughed once again, and Rollison laughed also as he moved with swift, almost startling speed, lifted her as if she were a casket of feathers, and stepped masterfully through the doorway.

Unfortunately, his path was not clear. He was barely across the threshold when his foot kicked something soft, not heavy, but heavy enough to trip him up and send him right off balance. Instinctively, he hugged Perdita more closely to him, staggering helplessly, not knowing whether he could save himself from pitching over.

The wild momentum slackened. A little less instinc-

9

tively he turned his shoulder to the wall. Still holding Perdita, he crashed into it, but apart from the shock of the impact, she came to no harm and he did no more than bruise himself. He lowered Perdita's feet to the floor, and for a few quivering seconds they clung together. Then drawing apart, they turned and looked down at the threshold.

He saw a bundle of rags, just inside the door.

So did Perdita.

Rollison ran his hand across his forehead, staring at the bundle, and asked in a low-pitched voice:

"Are you all right?"

"I'm fine," replied Perdita, shakily.

"I'm sorry if I shook you up."

"I can't imagine how you managed to keep on your feet."

"Luck," said Rollison; then in a mystified voice: "Look."

She was staring in the same direction as he, and as intently.

"Do you see what I see?" Rollison went on.

"It's a—blanket."

"It's a—bundle of rags."

"No," Perdita said, more sharply. "It's a shawl."

"A *what*?"

"It's a shawl," repeated Perdita in a sharper voice, and then added in sudden anxiety: "Oh, my goodness!"

She freed herself from Rollison's supporting arm and rushed back towards the door, dropping on one knee, a kind of urgency suddenly upon her.

Rollison followed, leaning over her as she unwrapped the bundle of rags which might be a shawl or even a blanket. Suddenly he saw the top of a tiny head and an unmistakable wisp of jet black hair.

"*No*," he breathed.

But even as astonishment gave way to shock, and shock to alarm, even as the first presentiment of catastrophe came to him, it was as if another part of him stood aside, marveling. The charming young widow, with all her brittle sophistication, was changing before his eyes. In place of the challenge to adventure, the awareness, the "I dare you" in her gaze, there was now all the selflessness, the yearning of a mother. She had forgotten Rollison. She had forgotten herself. She was aware only of this tiny infant. With infinite gentleness she put aside the rags. She did not look round, but said in a firm, decisive voice:

"Get some warm water, and some soft towels, then some hot-water bottles. Hurry please." Rollison stared as she looked down at the child, then slowly, carefully, lifted it to her bosom.

"Hurry," she repeated. "Please hurry."

He turned to the bathroom.

He was dazed and bewildered, but the habit of efficiency and of calm in the face of all emergencies very soon asserted itself. In the kitchen cupboard, he knew, there was a stack of fibreglass bowls, used by Jolly for various culinary purposes.

He removed several smaller bowls from a large one, half filled this with hot water, then tempered the hot with cold. Carrying it into the bathroom, he stood it on the W.C. pan and drew up a cork-topped stool. The airing cupboard was just outside the bathroom, and he took down a pile of towels and felt them for softness and thickness.

He heard Perdita, turned and saw her standing behind him, the baby in her arms.

"Is it ready?" she demanded.

"Yes. Everything all right?" Somehow he could not bring himself to frame the question which had sprung to his mind: "Is the child dead?"

"It's alive," she answered.

"Good!"

"Just," she qualified. "We must have a doctor."

11

"Or a nurse."

"I'm the nurse," said Perdita. She gave him a strangely piercing look. "Do you think your doctor will know anything about newborn babies?"

"Newborn——!" he stopped, aghast.

"Do you?"

"I can soon find out," he said.

"Do that," said Perdita, almost tartly.

She saw the bowl of water, and hesitated, Rollison stood with the towels in his hands, and Perdita suddenly thrust the baby at him, and said:

"Keep perfectly still."

She placed the baby on the towels he was carrying; Rollison could see a tiny, pink, wrinkled face—that, and the fluffy wisp of hair, was all that was visible. He stood motionless, almost fearful, while Perdita slipped off her sable wrap, put her hands to the back of her neck, unzipped, then, with a few quick movements, slipped out of her tight black evening dress. Taking a pale blue bathrobe from the back of the door, she put it on and knotted the sash. Then she moved past Rollison to the bowl of water and dipped the back of her hand into it.

"That's about right," she approved. "Let me have her."

Her?

Sitting on the stool, she placed the baby on her lap.

"Will you call the doctor, then get the bottles?" she asked.

"Yes," said Rollison. "Yes, I will." Once again, as she looked up at him, he noted that strangely penetrating glance.

Turning towards the sitting-room, he watched, at once fascinated and repelled, as Perdita began to unwrap the infant, glimpsing the rest of the tiny, pink face, the unbelievably wrinkled arms and shoulders, thinking, "It *can't* be alive." Reaching the telephone, he began to dial the doctor, who lived across the street, but suddenly he put

12

down the receiver, paused long enough to get the dialing tone and dialed a Mayfair number.

The ringing went on for a long time, and he began to fear that he was too late.

Then: "The Marigold Club," a woman answered.

"Is that Maria?" Rollison asked.

"Why, yes," the woman said, her voice warming. "How are you, Mr. Rollison?"

It might have been one o'clock in the afternoon, and not one o'clock in the morning.

"A very worried man," declared Rollison.

"Oh, I *am* sorry. Lady Gloria's away, you know, but if I can help——"

"Maria," Rollison interrupted, "a few months ago you had a spot of bother with a prematurely born child. Remember?"

"I do indeed!"

"And you rushed it to the hospital."

"It's a *beautiful* baby now," enthused Maria. "You ought to see——"

"If you had another one, how soon could you get the hospital alerted?"

"In a very few minutes," answered Maria. "I'd just telephone and ask for an ambulance with an incubator." She caught her breath. "But Mr. Rollison——"

"Did you take it to St. Mary's or did they send for it?"

"Oh, they sent an ambulance. But——"

"Telephone them straight away and tell them to send an ambulance and incubator to Gresham Terrace," pleaded Rollison. "Someone's left a newborn baby on my doorstep. And Maria—please ask them to hurry." He rang off on her hasty promise.

All at once he started, and stood motionless. His glance passed, unseeing, round the big living-room, past the wall covered with trophies of strange hunts and captures, past his large desk, coming finally to the open door, through

13

which streamed the light from the bathroom. It was warm, but not warm enough to explain the sweat on his forehead, which, after a sudden vivid flash of understanding, ran in tiny rivulets down his face.

Perdita's gaze had seemed almost accusing. Now, at last, he realized what suspicions had prompted it.

The unsaid words echoed through and through his head.

"But why should anyone leave a baby here, Richard, if it isn't yours?"

2

SUSPICION

As he stood there, sobered both by the incident and by this new thought, Rollison was scowling. He could hear the rustle of movements and a gentle splashing of water, followed by a murmuring or humming sound. Quite suddenly, he smiled, his spirits rising inexplicably. He tiptoed from the living-room and along the passage to the kitchen, filled two rubber hot-water bottles—kept, so his man insisted, for guests—and went back to the bathroom.

Perdita *was* crooning, but he still thought he could detect a note of tension in her manner. The smile faded from his lips, and a fresh encroachment of anxiety for the child dampened his newly found high spirits.

"How is he?" he inquired.

Perdita did not look round, but asked:

"Is the doctor coming?"

"An ambulance will soon be here from St. Mary's Hospital," Rollison said, handing her the bottles.

"*Ambulance?*"

"With an incubator or what-do-you-call-it," Rollison went on. "The quicker we can get the little beggar into expert hands, the better. How is he?"

"It's a girl," Perdita insisted. She was wrapping the child up in an enormous bundle of warm towels, one hot-water bottle near the top of the bundle, another near the bottom, making it look big and bulky. Rollison could just see the tiny head at the end of a gigantic cylindrical roll of white.

"Perdita," he said firmly, "I want to know how she is."

After a pause, Perdita swiveled round on the stool, looked at him squarely and said:

"Her heart's beating, but she's terribly frail. She can't

be more than a few hours old—a day at most. What a shocking thing to do." The words rapped out as if the plight of the tiny creature on her lap really wrung Perdita's heart. Rollison was annoyed with himself because his reactions had been so egotistical: how would this affect *him?* As he looked down on the woman with whom he had been dancing and laughing only a short while before, he was once again, amazed at the change in her.

He thought spontaneously: Mother and child.

Perdita asked sharply: "Why are you looking at me like that?"

It would be almost impossible, certainly unwise, to put his thoughts into words, so he said quite lightly:

"Even in my bathrobe, you're the loveliest woman I know."

Before she could respond, the front door bell rang.

"Could that be the ambulance?" Perdita asked.

"If it is, they've really got a move on," Rollison called over his shoulder.

They had indeed.

As he opened the door, a young doctor appeared, followed by two ambulance men carrying the incubator, complete with oxygen and a humidifier, blankets and hot-water bottles. They moved quickly and competently, taking complete control. The doctor lifted the child, glanced approvingly at Perdita, and said:

"I wish we always found them as well-cared for."

"*Always?*" echoed Perdita. "You mean this often happens?"

"Not exactly twice a night, but far too often," the doctor said. He placed the infant gently inside the incubator. "And far too often the police find only the bodies, or the skeletons. Peculiar things, people." He was about twenty-eight and fresh-faced, but his manner was that of one old and wearied in his contact with human nature. "Have you told the police, Mr. Rollison?"

"Not yet."

"We shall have to report it," the doctor said. He smiled at Perdita. "Thank you very much indeed." He turned, followed the two ambulance men towards the door, and for a moment it looked as if Perdita would let them go without a word. Then suddenly, she called:

"Doctor!"

He turned.

"Yes?"

"May I come and see how she's getting along?"

"Of course—any time." Suddenly the young man became a mischievous schoolboy, his eyes sparkled and his lips curved. "Just ask for the Toff's foundling."

He closed the door behind him, before either Rollison or Perdita had recovered. They stood staring at each other, close to the wall against which Rollison had thudded only a short time before.

Gradually Rollison began to smile.

"Nice young chap," he observed. "And very pleased with your efforts."

"Was he?" Perdita was half frowning. "I wonder whether"—she hesitated, and then went on under her breath—"if she will live."

"And what will become of her if she does," Rollison said. He put his arm affectionately around Perdita's shoulder, and led her into the living-room. "Sit here," he invited, pulling up a chair.

She dropped down into it, as if all the strength had suddenly gone out of her.

Rollison went to a Regency cupboard and opened it to a bewildering array of bottles and cut glass. He took out two brandy glasses, poured Courvoisier into each, cupping his hands about one glass for a few seconds and watching Perdita. She was sitting back in the chair, her legs stretched out, her arms limp in her lap. She was looking directly at him, but Rollison had the feeling that she was seeing someone or something else.

"Brandy?" he suggested at last.

17

"Thank you." She took the glass he handed to her, inhaled the bouquet and sipped mechanically. Rollison sat on a corner of his big desk, his broad shoulders framed by the Trophy Wall. For a few minutes neither spoke; it was that rare thing, a companionable silence. Gradually, life returned to Perdita's eyes, and color to her cheeks. At first, she had been limp; now she was merely relaxed.

Suddenly, she said:

"Villain."

"Have I ever denied it?"

"I'm sure you'll deny the implication of *this*."

"I'm going to be deliberately obtuse," said Rollison amiably.

"Perhaps you're wise." Perdita sipped again, and then announced with great deliberation: "I like you."

"I'm delighted."

"But not everybody likes you."

"Enough is enough."

Perdita laughed on a low note.

"Yes, I like you very much, although I don't usually like dark, wavy-haired men. Do women often say they like you?"

"Not women who have just saved a child's life," answered Rollison soberly.

"Oh, I didn't do anything. If only——"

"Not that!" interrupted Rollison urgently. "Not false modesty between us, please. You saved that child, and you know it."

"But supposing it doesn't survive?" Perdita frowned, sipped with fastidious delicacy again, then sat up a little. "Rolly—what are all those weapons behind you?"

"The tools of those who dislike me," Rollison answered.

"Seriously."

"I'm being very serious."

Perdita frowned again, this time in genuine puzzlement.

18

"You mean you really are what they say you are?"

"Who are 'they' and what do they say?"

"Everyone to whom I've talked about you," Perdita answered. "They say you're a kind of"—there was an infinitesimal pause, but it was long enough to convey a million doubts—"amateur detective."

"So I've been called," agreed Rollison.

"And that you sometimes work with the police at Scotland Yard."

"Or in spite of them."

Perdita's eyes were widening.

"Some called you a private eye, and some said you were an investigator. Others called you an inquiry agent, and—well, they all seemed to think you were a little mad and more than a little dangerous."

"And presumably that's why you accepted my invitation to dinner."

"*And* why I accepted your invitation to your apartment!"

"Knowing, of course, that you could look after yourself, whether or not I was the madman they hinted I was."

She laughed.

"You're absolutely delightful."

"You're absolutely honest," said Rollison.

"Is that intended as a compliment?"

"I can't think of a greater one."

"That's nice," remarked Perdita. She leaned back again, relaxed, without pose and very beautiful. "I can't think of anything nicer than being loved for my character instead of my looks."

"How about for your money?" Rollison asked drily.

"That, I don't believe—you're not a fortune hunter. I never knowingly accept an invitation with anyone who might be."

"How unadventurous! But perhaps you're wise." Rollison moved to the other side of the desk and contemplated the Trophy Wall, which was indeed a remarkable wall to behold. On it were dozens of trophies, each a memento of a case on which he had worked, a mystery which he had helped to solve. Some told a story of courage, some a story of danger, some a story of death—and all were proof of the Honorable Richard Rollison's skill in the art and science of detection. There was a lock of hair from a kidnapped child; a bloodstained feather; a silk stocking laddered by the nails of a strangler. There were knives and guns and blunt instruments, and there were poisons.

Rollison took a small hermetically sealed box of chocolates from a tiny shelf, and brought it to Perdita.

"These have been treated with preservatives to enable them to outlast me," he said. "The intention of the husband who gave them to his wife was that he should outlive her, and enjoy her fortune."

"And did he?" Perdita asked a little nervously.

"He outlived her by about six months, in the days when murderers were hanged."

Perdita gave a little shudder, then asked briskly: "How much did he stand to win?"

"Forty thousand pounds."

"She wasn't worth the risk; but I would be."

"Stop boasting of your millions."

"Did you catch him?"

"Yes."

"Why should it interest you?" When Rollison didn't answer, Perdita went on: "I don't mean the poor woman you've told me about, I mean investigating crime. Are you so bored with life in general?"

"I would be if I didn't specialize in the particular," said Rollison. "I don't really know why I am interested. Call it natural inquisitiveness, a love of second-hand excitement, or if you really want to go to town, even a streak of puritan morality—a kind of social conscience."

Perdita's eyes danced. "Hi, Puritan! Have you always been so interested in morality?"

"Since I first learned how unjust life can be," Rollison said, "and that was a long time ago. Will you have more brandy?"

"No, thank you," said Perdita. "I feel almost myself again, now. It *was* a bit of a shock." Her eyes mocked him. "This child really is a mystery you have to solve if you want to preserve your reputation for morality! Will you give me an honest answer to a simple question?"

"An honest one, or no answer at all."

She stared at him for what seemed a long time, and then asked quite clearly:

"Do you have any reason to believe the child is yours?"

Rollison had expected the question, had prepared himself for it, yet it caught him by surprise. One half of his mind had already perceived the devastating quality of honesty, of truthfulness in Perdita Shortt, but the other half had rejected the possibility that she would put it in such unequivocal words.

He answered with great deliberation.

"None whatsoever."

"Then why should anyone bring it here?" Perdita asked, now obviously becoming anxious, as well as perplexed.

"There are three possible reasons," Rollison enumerated briskly. "One, that someone thinks I am responsible. Two, that someone believes I'll look after the child and see that it gets a square deal. Three, that it's an effort to involve me in some kind of problem, probably in some kind of crime. If nothing develops in the next twenty-four hours or so, I'll put my money on the second possibility. Which do you think it is?"

"I don't know," said Perdita pensively, "but I know which I'd like it to be."

"Number three?"

"Of course! Think how exciting it would be!"

"I think you might react strongly against that kind of

excitement," Rollison said drily. "Perdita, my pet, if they run true to form the police will be here soon, and if the men of the Press run true to form, they'll be here soon afterwards. The police won't do any harm, but the Press might do no good to your reputation. Tomorrow's late editions would carry flaming headlines: *'Millionaire's Widow Cares for Toff's Foundling'*—that kind of thing." When Perdita made no comment, Rollison went on: "And they would go on to make it clear that you and I were together here in a compromising situation. The worst would undoubtedly be assumed."

"I don't think I care what people think," said Perdita, almost nonchalantly. "Do you?"

"What they think about you, yes."

"Richard, dear," said Perdita Shortt, "we must strike a bargain and shake hands and kiss on it. I will be honest with you if you will be honest with me. Right?"

"It would be an interesting experiment," said Rollison. "It could be devastating." He put out his hand, and Perdita took it; then he shifted his grip, and pulling her up from the chair, kissed her full on the lips. "Bargain sealed," he declared. "It remains a fact that I'm much more concerned for your reputation than I need be for my own. Everyone thinks the worst of me already. So, put on your dress, and——"

Before he could finish, while he was still holding her close, there was a sharp ring at the front door bell.

"It's too late," Perdita said. She did not look as if she were particularly perturbed. "I'll dress, you open the door."

3

PRESS?

As Rollison entered the lounge hall, he looked up at a spot above the front door, to a kind of periscope mirror built into the wall above the lintel by Jolly. Now reflected in the tiny mirror, Rollison could see two men, one of them carrying a camera. He recognized neither.

The two men put their heads together; whispering.

Rollison moved forward and opened the door. They drew a little apart, one tall, the other short and very thin; it was he who held the camera.

"Mr. Rollison?" asked the tall man.

"Yes."

"We're from the *Daily Globe*, Mr. Rollison. Can you spare a few minutes?"

Rollison did not move back to let them in.

"It's very late," he observed.

"Not so late as all that for the Toff!" jollied the tall man. "My name is Osgood, this is Punchy Parks. We won't keep you long." He moved forward, but Rollison still blocked his path. They stood close together, face to face, as Osgood went on: "Whose baby was it, do you know?"

"What baby?" inquired Rollison, poker-faced.

"I think you know the baby I'm talking about, sir. The one that's being looked after at St. Mary's Hospital." Osgood moved swiftly to one side, the gaze of his rather pale grey eyes shifting all the time, as if for some kind of evidence, perhaps some sign of someone else at the flat. "Not every day of the week a baby gets left on the Toff's doorstep! Who picked it up? You, or the lady?"

Rollison asked gently: "What lady?"

"Now that's going too far," protested Osgood. "We

had a word with one of the ambulance men, just a few simple questions and answers. You can't fool me, Mr. Rollison. I know about the baby and I know about the lady."

Rollison was strongly tempted to hit him. Instead, he moved past him towards the big room, which was empty, speaking in an even voice from which very little could be deduced.

"Before I do anything else I have to make a phone call." He stepped to his desk and stood by the telephone; the door leading to the bathroom and bedroom was closed, and Perdita was making no sound. Both men followed him. There was a glint in the photographer's eyes at sight of the Trophy Wall.

Rollison dialed.

The camera clicked.

Rollison heard the ringing tone on the telephone.

Osgood went closer to the Trophy Wall, as if it had drawn all interest in the baby out of him.

"*Daily Globe*," an operator said.

"Mr. Wiseman, please," said Rollison, glancing at Osgood, who must have heard him but who still appeared to be hypnotized by the Trophies.

"Who wants him, please?"

"Richard Rollison."

"One moment, sir."

As he stood waiting, Rollison watched Osgood edging closer to the passage door, and he had little doubt that the man would soon open it. There was the other possibility, that Perdita would open it from the other side; that would cause quite a situation.

A man said briskly into his ear: "What can I do for you, Rolly?"

"Tell me if you employ a reporter named Osgood and a camera-man named Parks, Punchy Parks," said Rollison, speaking very close to the telephone.

24

"What's that?" There was a pause, before Wiseman's voice rose: "*What* names did you say?"

"Osgood and Parks."

"I don't know what you're getting at," said Wiseman, whom the Toff knew well, "but the answer is no. And if they say they've come to see you from the *Globe*, they're liars whatever their names are. I'd have been told at once if we'd sent anyone to you—hold on a sec!"

That was the moment when Osgood stretched out and touched the handle of the passage door. As he did so he glanced over his shoulder, to see if Rollison noticed, but Rollison appeared to be absorbed in the telephone conversation. Osgood turned the handle.

Rollison roared: "Come away from there!"

The photographer gasped. Osgood snatched his fingers from the handle and spun round, the door still closed. Moving with bewildering speed, Rollison caught Osgood's arm and flung him to one side. Following this up, he gripped Osgood's arm again, thrust it behind him in a hammer-lock, and hustled him towards the front door, which was still open. The photographer was making protesting noises, but taking no action.

Rollison pulled the front door wide open, and hurtled Osgood out. Little Punchy Parks darted past him as if he couldn't move fast enough, and Rollison let him go unscathed. He slammed the door on them, then stood back and looked up at the periscope mirror. As he did so there was a movement behind him, and he caught a whiff of familiar perfume.

"What are you staring at?" Perdita demanded in a whisper.

Rollison picked up the telephone in time to hear Wiseman saying: "No one's phoned in a story about you—or asked to hold space for you. What——"

"Thanks," said Rollison. "I'll be in touch." He put down the telephone, and moved to one side, then stepped

25

behind Perdita, guiding her head so that she looked up and saw the tiny reflection of the men outside. She caught her breath, but did not speak. Rollison put his face very close to hers, so that he, also, could see. Osgood seemed to be straightening his clothes; the little man was staring up at him intently.

Then Osgood took his right hand out of his pocket.

"*Look!*" gasped Perdita. "He's got a gun!"

"We'll have to be careful, won't we," Rollison said. "Watch."

Osgood was moving towards the front door, and Punchy Parks was talking urgently, looking anxiously up into his face, and tugging at his sleeve. No one could doubt that Osgood wanted to return to the attack, by breaking in, or waiting for someone to come out, and the photographer was trying desperately to prevent him.

Suddenly, their attitudes changed. They sprang apart, Osgood thrusting the gun into his pocket, Parks standing as if to attention. A moment later the figure of a policeman, infinitesimally small in the mirror, appeared on the landing below.

"*Well!*" breathed Perdita.

"I can't follow our phoney newspapermen, but at least we can now relax," said Rollison, and he led her back towards the living-room. She was fully dressed again, even to the sable wrap. "You look more wonderful than ever," he told her. "Make yourself at home."

As he spoke, there was a ring at the front door bell, and he left Perdita and turned to open the door. Before he touched it he glanced at the mirror, to make sure that the self-styled newspapermen had gone. Then he opened the door to a burly, middle-aged police sergeant, who gave a beaming smile.

"*Good*-evening, sir!"

"Hallo, hallo," said Rollison. "Nice to see a familiar face. Come in." He led the way to the living-room, where Perdita was standing by the Trophy Wall, her hand stretched towards the box of chocolates. She glanced round. "Mrs. Shortt," Rollison said, "the law's come to talk to you about our baby. Meet Police Sergeant Wills."

"*Our* baby, sir?" ejaculated Sergeant Wills. Then hurriedly: "Oh, I see, sir—Mrs. Shortt was with you when you found it. Ha—Ha! If you would be good enough to give me the details . . . Yes, a whisky and soda would be very welcome, Mr. Rollison, very kind of you . . . Your very good health, Mrs. Shortt. Now, if you'll tell me just what happened——"

Perdita watched in fascination as the sergeant's stodgy, blunt-tipped fingers guided a yellow ball-point pen in bewilderingly fast shorthand. Now and again he sipped his drink, now and again he shot her a questioning glance for confirmation, but generally it was a steady flow. When at last the whole story had been told, he finished his drink, then read the statement back with hardly a pause.

"Word perfect," congratulated Rollison."

"Wonderful!" applauded Perdita.

"Very kind of you," said Sergeant Wills. "Just one thing, sir. How was it you didn't see the baby before you stumbled over it?"

There was a moment of silence. In it, Rollison and Perdita looked at each other, and after a second, understanding dawned on the sergeant.

"I *see*, sir. You were both looking elsewhere!" He made a note, as the others laughed, remembering their mood.

"I'll have it typed out, and send a copy through for you to sign in the morning. Now if I could have the shawls, sir, and anything else that came with the baby, so to speak, I'll be on my way."

"Have you any idea who left the child?" Perdita inquired.

"Can't say we have yet, ma'am, but we might pick up

some news during the night. And we'll be after your neighbors in the morning, to find out if anyone saw anything. Sorry business, though. Never know whether to hope the poor little basket'll live or die."

Perdita looked stonily ahead of her. When Rollison came back from seeing Sergeant Wills out, she was speaking into the telephone.

"Yes . . . Yes, that's right . . . Yes, please." She paused turning to Rollison. "I'm speaking to the hospital. I didn't think I'd come to *hate* your friend Sergeant Wills, but how can anyone be so callous? I . . . *Hallo?*" Her voice, her eyes, her whole body, seemed suddenly to come alive. "Yes . . . oh, *thank* you, thank you very much." She rang off and turned to the Toff, her face radiant. "She's holding her own!"

"I have a feeling she's going to prove a tough little brat," said Rollison.

"Don't *you* start being callous."

"Oh, I'm not callous," Rollison assured her. "I simply want to know who she is, who brought her here and——"

Yet another ring at the front door bell interrupted him, and obviously disappointed Perdita, who frowned as she looked towards the door. As he moved away, Rollison smiled at her, and said mildly:

"You'll have to make up your mind whether to stay here or leave, the excitement's only just beginning."

"Beginning?"

"Before you know where you are the telephone will start ringing and every newspaper and magazine from the *Guardian* to *Playboy* will beg some little tidbit we forgot to tell the others."

On the word "others" the telephone bell rang.

"Richard," Perdita said, forthrightly, "I've decided to stay."

"You're very welcome," Rollison said.

28

At the front door was an earnest middle-aged man from the *Globe*, with Mr. Wiseman's deep apologies and an urgent request for a description of the two men who had falsely claimed to represent his newspaper. The telephone call was from the British Broadcasting Corporation News Section, who had been told . . . Hardly had the door closed and the telephone receiver been replaced than there were more urgent callers. Cameras clicked and pencils slipped smoothly over paper. Men and women asked an astonishing variety of questions, from "What was the color of the baby's eyes?" to "Had Mrs. Shortt any children of her own?" Everyone wanted to know how much the baby weighed and whether it was dark, fair or between colors.

"Didn't see any resemblance to anyone did you, Mrs. Shortt?" asked a melancholy-looking, nearly bald Scotsman, with studied carelessness.

"As a matter of fact, I did," said Perdita, solemnly.

The Scotsman and three other reporters showed a swift revival of interest, and it could hardly be coincidence that each of them shot a surreptitious glance at Rollison.

"*Who* the Scotsman demanded.

"One of the Beatles," Perdita answered, still straight-faced. "It was something about the baby's hair——"

They laughed and took their leave. For the first time for over an hour, silence fell on Rollison's flat. He and Perdita were still in the living-room, sitting amid the debris of beer and Coca-Cola bottles, glasses and bottles of hard liquor. Perdita looked tired, almost exhausted, but she also looked content.

"Bed's the place for you," declared Rollison. "There's a double lock on the spare-room door for the timid and righteous." It was superfluous to add that the spare room had been sound-proofed, years ago, to make sure that no guest could be disturbed by the noises of the flat, or be aware of some of the strange and often noisy goings-on which were inseparable from the Toff's activities.

"What time is it?" asked Perdita. She glanced at her watch, exclaiming: "Goodness! It's getting on for three." She struggled up from her chair.

Twenty minutes later, Rollison tried the handle of her door; she was neither timid nor righteous. In fact, she was already sleeping, her clothes on a chair at the foot of the bed. Rollison closed the door gently, and went to his own room.

It was amazing how much he missed the ministrations of Jolly, and how tired he was; *anno domini* had to be reckoned with. He got into bed, closed his eyes, hoping he would fall asleep right away, but he did not. Time and time again he felt as if he were falling, with Perdita in his arms; and time and time again he saw in his mind's eye, that pink, wrinkled face.

Who had brought the infant here? And *why?*

At heart, he did not believe it was simply a case of a desperate mother coming to a place where she felt she could rely on human kindness. Who, wishing to abandon the child, would break into a house and walk up three long flights of stairs? Certainly not a distraught unmarried mother, weak after the agony and anguish of childbirth. Someone strong and healthy must have climbed those stairs; and in any case, a professional criminal must surely have opened the street door. If there were any doubts about such reasoning, there were none about the visit of Osgood and Punchy Parks, and none about Osgood's anger or his gun, or the chances of him being a professional criminal.

Rollison began to doze, trying to stem the continual speculation.

At last he feel asleep; and slept soundly, free from dreams.

In that flat in the heart of London there was absolute

quiet. Outside it was quiet, too, except for the sound of an occasional taxi engine, or the plodding of a policeman on his rounds. Soon after six o'clock, dawn broke and London stirred; the noise became more frequent, more persistent, milkmen and postmen and newspaper-boys peopled the streets.

At seven there came the roar of a powerful motorcycle engine as it turned into Gresham Terrace. The rider was a young man, bare-headed, black-haired and wild-eyed.

He hurtled down the street, jammed on the brakes and slid to a standstill one door away from Number 22. He leapt off the machine and propped it up on its stand in a swift succession of movements which made it seem as if he was operated by remote control. A youth with a red-painted bicycle and an enormous canvas bag filled with newspapers gazed with sudden rapture at the royal blue magnificence of this B.S.A. motorcycle; an elderly milkman at the wheel of an electric float, bottles rattling and clinking, stared at the youth, noticing those wild eyes, the pallor, the quivering tension at the full fine lips.

The young man reached the front door of Number 22, which by day was left unlocked, so that there was easy access to all the flats, secure in their own stout locks and bolts. He flung it open and rushed up the stairs, iron tips at the heels and the toes of his shoes ringing out a kind of hymn of hate; sparks actually flew from them.

He paused long enough to glance at the name at each door, before reaching the top. There was Rollison's name on a discreet little panel, and the young man started to ring the bell, bang at the door and shout, all at the same time.

"Rollison!" he bellowed. "Rollison! Come out here, I want to see you!"

4

OUTRAGED YOUTH

Rollison heard the hullaballoo through the mists of reluctant waking. His head and his eyes were heavy, the last thing he wanted to do was wake, but the din kept on and on, pierced by the penetration of the bell. After two or three minutes he dragged himself out of bed and groped for a dressing-gown, already missing Jolly, who would normally have dealt with such a situation. He was almost forgetful of what had happened until he passed the spare room. Glancing at the closed door, he smiled with an affection rare in him, then quickened his pace as the knocking became heavier. Pictures and ornaments shook, and now Rollison was wide enough awake to be annoyed.

He glanced up at the periscope mirror as for a split second silence fell, and saw the youth outside. But the reflection did not show his pallor, nor the fury in his expression. It did show the way he threw back his head and roared:

"Open the bloody door or I'll break it down!"

Rollison opened the door just as the youth began to beat at it again, this time with clenched fists. In consequence he staggered forward, his fists falling lightly against Rollison's chest instead of on the wooden panels. For a moment, his loss of balance bewildered him, but he drew back swiftly.

"Are you Rollison?"

"Yes." Rollison had just time to see the rage in the red-rimmed eyes and to recognize the signs of an emotional storm, before the youth launched himself forward, fists still clenched and flung at Rollison's face.

Rollison quickly recognized another fact; this youth

was a trained fighter. Even in his rage he dropped into the right stance. Rollison bent his head, and a right fist hurtled past; he ducked, and caught the left. Now he was really angry. Closing with his assailant, he put his arms round him, hugged tightly enough to squeeze the breath out of his lungs, then hurtled him back against the open door. He heard the thwack of the dark head on the wood, saw the eyes roll, the body crumple up. Like an actor in a film shown in slow motion, the youth slid to the floor.

Rollison looked down at him dispassionately, all anger gone. He was glad of the respite, and hoped that the bang on the head hadn't done much harm. He bent over the youth, but found no sign of injury; the breathing was a little heavy, but seemed regular.

He studied the pale face, and noticed the curling black lashes, showing vividly against the pallor of the cheeks. The boy was handsome in a lean, rather Southern European way, with beautifully formed lips. His chin was square and broad; even as it sagged against his chest, it gave him a look of strength. He wore tight-fitting blue jeans and a shiny black leather jacket which was zipped up to his neck.

Rollison had a quick bath, dressed, shaved, then went along to the kitchen and plugged in the electric kettle. He paused outside Perdita's door, but there was no sound. Back in the kitchen he made tea, and put two cups on a tray by the time he heard heavy footsteps. A moment later the youth appeared in the doorway. He seemed dazed, but glowered as if the anger was still in him, and likely to erupt at the slightest provocation.

"Cup of tea?" invited Rollison brightly. "Cold wash?" The youth glared at him, and his eyes, though red-rimmed and bloodshot, were chestnut brown and beautiful. Rollison poured tea into two cups. "Milk and sugar?"

The youth opened his mouth, then closed it again.

"Help yourself," said Rollison.

"You swine," growled the youth.

"Sticks and stones," murmured Rollison. The hot tea was good. "What's all this about?"

"You know what it's about."

"I certainly don't."

"You flicking liar!"

"You know, I don't like being called a liar," Rollison said, a steely note creeping into his voice. "I shouldn't say that again."

"You're a flicking liar! You seduced my sister and then you let her down. Why, I——"

Rollison looked at the youth long and levelly, and then struck him. The boy realized what was coming, snatched up the cup of hot tea Rollison had pushed towards him and flung it across the room. Most of it flew over Rollison's head, only a few drops stung his face. He saw the youth spring to a defensive position, and knew something had to be done quickly if he was to make sure he didn't come off the loser. He put in a straight left which the other brushed aside, geared himself to a supreme effort, then heard Perdita exclaim:

"Richard!"

She was in the doorway, flushed and lovely with her hair awry and eyes rounded. She wore a fluffy, pale pink dressing-gown, taken from the spare room wardrobe.

Rollison dropped his guard.

"Good morning," he said. "You're just in time for tea."

He kept a sharp eye on the youth, fearing he might leap into attack now that his adversary was unprepared. For a moment it looked as if he would do that, but something stopped him.

Momentarily reassured, Rollison poured out a third cup of tea, but as he handed it to Perdita, who advanced slowly into the kitchen, the youth once again braced his shoulders and clenched his fists.

"You're not going to get away with it," he shouted.

"With what?" inquired Perdita. "What on *earth* is all this about?"

"*He* knows."

"I only know that our young friend thinks that I've fathered his sister's child, which isn't true."

"You mean your—your *sister's* the baby's mother?" cried Perdita, and she nearly dropped her cup in excitement. "Why, that's——Richard! Have you telephoned the hospital yet?"

"I've hardly had time to——"

"Never mind! Where's your sister?" demanded Perdita, eagerly.

"I don't know," the youth replied, and suddenly he appeared to be pathetic. "She's not at home. She's not with any of her friends. I'm worried stiff about her," he added miserably.

"So I should think! But Mr. Rollison will find her," Perdita said imperiously. "I must find out how the baby is."

She did not wait for a reply, but turned and hurried out of the kitchen. The youth, bewildered, for a moment was suddenly touched by her excitement. He stared after her.

"What did she mean about a baby?"

"I'll ask the questions," Rollison said, firmly. "Who are you?"

"Never mind!"

"Give me your name and answer my questions or I'll send for the police and charge you with assault," Rollison insisted. "Who are you?"

The youth did not fight very hard this time.

"My name's Bishop. Syd Bishop," he muttered.

"What's your sister's name?"

"As if you didn't know!"

"I'll ram your teeth down your throat if you don't answer me!"

35

"I'd like to see you try." There was less anger in Syd Bishop's tone, however, and he seemed to relax, as if he were satisfied with question and answer for the time being. "Her name's Betty—*and* you know it."

"Betty Bishop?"

"Yes! Listen, I——"

"When did she have this baby?"

"Last—last night, I think. And when I heard about *your* baby—in the paper——"

"Where was Betty's baby born?"

"I don't know. I didn't know it was so near. I was out yesterday, had to bring a new car down from Coventry. When I got home she was out. My Dad didn't know where she was, the drunken old so-and-so. I've been up all night trying to find her. *Where is she?*" Now anger was back in his voice—anger and determination.

"We'll find out," said Rollison confidently, although he had no idea where to begin looking. "Have you reported her missing?"

"Who would I report to?"

"The police, of course."

"Are you crazy?" Bishop demanded shrilly.

Rollison said: "It's crazy not to tell them, but forget it for a moment. I found a newborn baby in the doorway here last night, and it was rushed to hospital. Mrs. Shortt's gone to find out how it is this morning. That's all I know."

"You're a flicking——"

"Hold it!" said Rollison sharply. "You're becoming monotonous."

Bishop hesitated, looked as if the word "liar!" was going to burst from his lips again, but somehow forced it back. Before Rollison could go on, Perdita came hurrying in, her face bright, her eyes glowing.

"She's doing well," she announced.

"*She?*" echoed Bishop.

"It looks as if you've got a niece," Rollison told him

drily. "Perdita, put the kettle on if you want to make more tea. Syd Bishop, I need some more information, but first there's something you have to get into your head. I don't know your sister. I've never heard of——"

"Shut your big mouth," Bishop interrupted, harshly. "Look at *this*." He fumbled with the zipper of a pocket, took out a wallet, opened the wallet and took out a photograph, which he thrust in front of Rollison. It was the picture of a girl, probably in her late teens; an attractive girl who was remarkably like Syd Bishop. "Now tell me you don't know her!"

Rollison studied the photograph closely and for a long time. At last he handed it to Perdita, then looked straight into Bishop's eyes and declared:

"I have never seen her in my life."

He half expected the youth to lose his temper again, but Bishop controlled himself, moistened his lips and stared back intently, as if he thought that by outstaring the Toff, he could judge his truthfulness.

"It's true, you know," Rollison said quietly. "Whoever told you that I knew her was the liar."

There was a moment's silence.

"My—God!" breathed Bishop.

"Who was it?" asked Rollison.

"The *swine*."

"Who?"

"Just wait until I get at him!"

"If he's the man I think he is, he'll shoot you in the back," Rollison said.

"*Shoot?*"

"With a gun. Bang bang."

"That's not funny! He—he's a chap I know."

"A friend?"

"Friend my titfer."

Perdita, who had been looking from one to the other, as if she were watching a game of table tennis, now gave an exclamation, making both men glance at her. The

37

pause gave Rollison time to reflect on what Syd Bishop had been saying, and to come to the conclusion that there was a great deal about the young man that he liked.

"What is a titfer?" Perdita inquired mildly.

"A hat," answered Rollison.

"Where d'you come from if you don't know what a titfer is?" demanded Bishop. Then he turned to Rollison, his hands bunched as if he were aching for action.

"Who is it?" Rollison demanded.

"He's a chap at the Club."

"What Club?"

"Mallow's Boxing Club," Bishop answered. "Don't tell me you've never heard of it."

"I know Mallow's," said Rollison. In fact, he was familiar with most of the clubs and gymnasiums in the East End of London, and patron to some of the best known. Mallow's was in Aldgate, not very far from the High Street, and one he did not greatly like. "Is this man a boxer?"

"He used to be."

"What's his name?"

"Osgood."

That was the first time since they had started question and answer that Rollison was taken by surprise, for it suggested that the man who had pretended to be from the *Globe* had, in fact, given his real name, when it would have been more in keeping with the circumstances had he given a false one.

"What's eating you?" demanded Bishop.

"Do you know a man named Parks?" asked Rollison.

"Punchy and Osgood," said Bishop. "They often pair up, them two. *You* know them?"

"I became acquainted last night." Rollison explained a little, and in the course of the explanation, the youth relaxed. Perdita nodded her head towards the passage and the sitting-room. "Good idea," Rollison said. "Let's go

38

and sit in comfortable chairs. If my man were here, he'd get us some breakfast."

"If that's a hint, forget it," Perdita said. "I don't want to miss a syllable of all this." She looked hard at Bishop, her expression almost as maternal as it had been when she had bathed the foundling infant. "Are you hungry, Syd?"

Bishop looked surprised.

"I suppose I am," he answered, vaguely. "I didn't have any supper last night."

"Then stay in here and I'll cook you some bacon and eggs while you're talking." Discovering one of Jolly's carpenters' aprons hanging behind the door, Perdita unhooked it, and put it on quite naturally, as if she was accustomed to kitchen chores. She opened the door of the refrigerator.

"Ossy told me he knew you'd got Betty into trouble," Bishop continued, turning to Rollison, hostility storming back to his face and eyes. "I phoned to ask if he knew where Betty was, and he told me she'd told him. Why the hell should he blame you if it's not true?"

5

HELP?

Perdita paused in the act of cracking eggs into the frying-pan, and Bishop stared with a "now get yourself out of that" challenge.

"Well, why *should* this man Osgood blame you?" Perdita demanded.

"That's what I want to find out," said Rollison, his voice hardening. "In fact, that's what I'm going to find out. How well do you know Osgood and Parks?"

"I see them around."

"How often?"

"Two or three nights a week at the Club or at a pub."

"How well do they know Betty?"

"She works at the same place as Ossy," Bishop answered. "She's a seamstress at a wholesale tailor's place in Houndsditch, and he's the foreman in the machine shop. They see each other most days, quite a lot, really. That's why I phoned him."

"Where does she work?" inquired Rollison.

"Ticky's."

"Ticky's what?"

"Ticky's Gown and Mantle Manufacturers, of course," answered Bishop, as if he could not understand the need for such a question. "You can't miss it. Why?"

"It's always wise to know," Rollison said, disarmingly. "When did you last see your sister?"

"Yesterday morning," Bishop told him. "I knew she was near her time, but I didn't expect it so soon. I wish to hell I knew where she was!" He swung round to Perdita. "You say the kid's okay?"

"The hospital just told me so."

"I'd hate anything to happen to that kid," Bishop said,

fervently. "She wanted it so bad. Wouldn't tell me anything about it, she wouldn't. Worked right up to the last minute, too. My God, if anything's happened to her——"

"Syd," said Rollison, "we're going to have breakfast, and then we're going to find out if Betty's back. If she isn't, we'll have to tell the police."

"I don't want any coppers——"

"What's your gripe against the police?" Rollison interrupted sharply. "You haven't got a record, have you?"

"I've never been inside, but that doesn't make me a pal of the cops."

"You might find out that they're better friends than Osgood and Parks," Rollison said. "There's a good fifty-fifty chance that those two know where Betty is . . . and an equal one that they brought the baby here, and came to make sure we'd found it. Almost certainly your sister didn't bring it. Few women could climb those stairs a few hours after having a child. . . ."

"Someone who'd handled babies wrapped the shawl round it," Perdita interjected. "No man did it so expertly."

"Unless he'd been trained in baby care," Rollison said, absently. He went on talking and reasoning, oblivious of the effect that his assumptions and his grasp of the situation were having on his listeners. Twice Syd Bishop gave Perdita an enormous wink, a sure indication that he was feeling better. Once Perdita raised her hands in front of her, in a kind of surrender.

Soon the kitchen was filled with the appetizing smell of bacon, and all three sat down to steaming plates. Five minutes later, Perdita said ruefully:

"If that's how you eat when you just *suppose* you're hungry, I wouldn't like to feed you when you're ravenous."

"You're not a bad cook, ma'am, I'll say that for you,"

praised young Bishop. "How soon do we start, Mr. Rollison?"

"In a very few minutes," Rollison answered.

In fact, they went out just before eight o'clock, leaving Perdita with two morning newspapers and their screaming headlines. It was a morning when there was little news, and the Toff and the Foundling filled the gap. Outside a youthful-looking policeman was inspecting the motor-cycle, as if with envy.

"Not going to leave it there long, are you?" he asked.

"Just off," said Bishop bluffly. "Coming with me, Mister?"

"Take me round to my garage," Rollison said. "Then I'll follow you home."

A dozen people, including several neighbors, watched with amazement as the elegant Mayfair-ite and the leather-jacketed youth went off together, Rollison straddling the pillion as if he revelled in the air rushing past his face and the bump-bump-bumpety-bump along the road. Soon he was at his garage, in Shepherd Market. Jolly had taken the runabout, an Austin, so Rollison unlocked the door of his magenta-red Bentley Continental.

"Cor!" exclaimed Bishop. "You're not coming in *that!*"

"Lead the way," ordered Rollison.

The Bentley caused no surprise in Mayfair or the City, but when Rollison turned off Whitechapel Road into the narrow back streets and the new building estates, the gleaming, magenta-red body, the glistening chromium, making an almost startling splash of color in the grey drabness of London's East End, many envious, wondering eyes followed him.

. Word soon spread that the Toff was paying a visit, and the news soon reached the police. It also reached men planning crimes to be carried out that very night. It reached the old and the young, the innocent and the guilty, and everywhere it carried excitement in its wake.

For here the Toff was known to every man, woman and child; and known to each, according to his conscience, as a man to dread, or as a man to revere.

At last Bishop turned into a narrow drab roadway where tiny terraced houses stood jammed like graying teeth in an enormous jaw. This was Gill Street. Each doorway opened straight on to the pavement, each house had a narrow door and single window, exactly like its neighbour. At frugal intervals lamps lined the kerb, like posts of a fence long since demolished. The street looked old and shabby and a little mean, without the dignity which age sometimes confers. At the far end, a crane and bull-dozer were groaning and creaking under a billow of dust. High above the grey slate roofs of the houses stood new blocks of flats, built of yellow brick and painted in bright colors—as if a new world were being created, gradually eating into the old one and crumbling it away.

Bishop stopped his machine just beyond a lamp post, halfway along. The sun shone on the sheen of his jacket and on his dark, wavy hair. And it reflected from the window of the house, outside of which he stopped.

Rollison noticed all of these things.

Others noticed the Toff and the Bentley. From along the street three schoolboys, caps askew and satchels swinging from their shoulders, started to run forward as if in a race.

"*It's a Bentley!*"

"*It's a Jag!*"

"*It's a Bristol, you silly mug!*"

Two schoolgirls, close by, drew up and looked searchingly at Rollison; one of them smiled boldly, while the other noticed the little monogram on the car door panel. This was a drawing of a man without a face, wearing a top hat, a monocle and a bow tie, and with a cigarette sticking out jauntily from a holder. The boys clattered up.

"Coo, look!"

"It's the *Toff!*"

As the soubriquet was uttered in a clear treble voice and the boys looked at Rollison as if at a sporting idol, people within earshot stopped to stare. One man very slender, with sloping shoulders and a slight hump, averted his eyes and scurried across the road. Rollison saw him, caught a glimpse of his profile and realized that it was Osgood's companion of the previous night—Punchy Parks. Rollison had neither time nor chance to follow him. Two heavily built men, swinging along like sergeant majors, eager for the parade ground, paused and stared. Several motorists slowed down as they passed the Bentley.

Syd Bishop, apparently oblivious of all these things, opened the door of the house, which had the number 53 painted in white over the letter-box. Already Rollison had noticed that the curtains as well as the window were clean, and a cactus, not the Victorian aspidistra, stood in the place of honour.

Bishop called: "I'm back, Pop."

There was no answer.

"Pop, I'm back!"

There was still no answer.

"The old beggar's sleeping it off," Bishop remarked, unable to keep a note of disgust out of his voice. "He'll be pickled when he goes to his own funeral."

He stepped into a tiny square of space at the foot of a flight of narrow steps. These, as well as the front door itself, led into a box-like parlour, much better furnished than might have been expected.

Rollison closed the door on the faces of half a dozen gaping passers-by.

"Pop!" yelled Bishop.

There was no answering sound, and he shrugged impatiently and started for the stairs; they were covered with wine-red haircord, and the walls had recently been distempered a pale grey.

Halfway up, Bishop changed his mind.

"Let him sleep," he said aloud.

"If your sister were here, where would she be?" demanded Rollison.

"In here—the stairs got a bit too much for her." Bishop came down the last few steps and walked through the parlour, pushing past the chairs arranged in front of the television set, and coming to a door at the far side. Rollison, following him, saw that this led into another room, which, in turn, led into the kitchen.

He stood with Bishop in the doorway.

On one side was a narrow bed, flush with the wall; on the other, a table and chair. The bed was unmade, but the clothes were neatly rolled back, the pillows uncreased. A pair of shoes stood beneath the chair, each shoe placed carefully one beside the other. On padded hangers, hooked over a rail set diagonally across the corner by the foot of the bed, hung two dresses, two or three skirts and a heavy cloth coat. On the table were several jars and bottles of make-up, arranged in rows, the tallest at the back. So Betty Bishop was a tidy person, reflected Rollison.

"When did you last see her?" he asked again.

"Six o'clock yesterday morning. I took her a cup of tea and a biscuit, like I always do. She said she wasn't feeling so good and I made her promise not to go to work."

"Was anyone else here?"

"Only Pop, upstairs. He was asleep, the old flicker, he never gets up until ten o'clock if he can help it. Lives on us, he does." There was now no doubt of the resentment in the lad's attitude towards his father. "Told her not to try to take his breakfast up, too." Bishop moved through to the kitchen, and his lips tightened. The sink was filled to overflowing with dirty cups and saucers, knives and forks, small saucepans and the debris of two or three meals. "So he got his own dinner *and* his own supper. Betty would have washed up."

Rollison said: "So she probably went off before lunch."

"Could have."

Rollison took stock of the crockery.

"Two of most things," he remarked. "One lot for your father at one meal, one for another. How do you get on with your neighbors?"

"The Cottons that way"—Bishop cocked a finger to the left—"are sons of bitches, but the Hendersons"—he cocked a finger in the other direction—"they're okay."

"Didn't they come in to see your sister sometimes?"

"We didn't exactly tell the world what she'd been up to," said Bishop drily. "But Ma Henderson knew."

"Did she see Betty leave, I wonder?"

"I dunno."

"You could ask."

"Well——"

"Do you want to find your sister, or don't you?"

There was a moment's pause.

"All right," Bishop muttered, "I'll go and see her."

"Syd——"

"Yes."

"Wouldn't your father know when Betty left?"

"When I come in he was in bed, sleeping it off—I yelled at him, but he didn't wake up. He's often like that." There was a pause. "I'll go and see Ma Henderson," Bishop added abruptly. He stepped to the door, hesitated and then turned round.

It was a strange and affecting moment. He looked so handsome, so young and so frightened. The shadows somehow heightened the glassiness and the redness of his eyes. He stood erect, with one hand stretched out as if pleading. When he spoke, his voice was gruff.

"Nothing could have happened to her, could it?"

It would be easy to utter a glib reassurance, thought Rollison, but would that help? Might it not, in fact, do positive harm? At least at the moment, Syd had respect

46

for, and perhaps some faith in, him. Speaking quietly, measuredly, he turned to meet the boy's anxious gaze.

"That's what we're going to find out, Syd. And it's why we may need to go to the police."

Bishop's eyes switched from Rollison to the stairs, as if he were looking through the ceiling and floor to the old man upstairs.

"He'll hate your guts if you do."

"I'll risk that," Rollison said drily. "Find out everything Mrs. Henderson or any of the other neighbors know, then come and tell me when it was that Osgood named me as the villain."

"On the phone. I told you. He was at a caff where we often have breakfast. He made a few nasty remarks about Betty, and then he said if I wanted to know who the father was, he'd tell me for a fiver—he said Betty had told him. If I'd been there I'd have knocked his teeth down his throat. When he told me I come rushing round here to see Betty, and when she wasn't here I come to see you."

"Thanks," said Rollison.

"If you're lying," Bishop said in the ferocious voice of very young manhood, "I'll ram *your* teeth down *your* throat. Don't make any mistake."

He flung himself out of the house, slamming the door so hard that the walls seemed to shake.

Rollison turned away and went upstairs. He was anxious to find out what the neighbors would say, but even more he wanted to talk to Pop. Obviously the youth was half frightened as well as resentful of his father, and ten minutes alone with the older man might yield more information than a long session with Syd. Rollison's shoulders touched the walls on either side of the narrow staircase. Soon it opened into a bedroom without a wall at the bannister side, almost filled with an old-fashioned double bed. Through a half-open door in the opposite wall Rollison saw the foot of another bed, rumpled bedclothes and, on the floor, a pair of shabby gray trousers which looked as if their wearer had simply loosened them, let them fall about his feet, and stepped clear.

Rollison crossed the first room, and pushed the door wider open.

A man was lying on the bed, his eyes staring towards the ceiling. He seemed strangely still.

There was a single gash across his throat.

The odd, the awful, the strangely nauseating thing, was that apart from a dark-red patch on the pillow on either side of his neck, there was no sign of blood.

6

POLICE

For some seconds, perhaps for a full minute, Rollison stood in the doorway. He felt numbed with shock. He was aware of voices in the street, of a car engine, of someone laughing on a raucous note, but here there was just the stillness of death.

At last, he moved slowly forward.

Because, over the years, he had trained his mind to search for clues, he looked for the knife, but saw none; looked for anything which might help in finding the killer, but noticed nothing at all. It was easy to believe that this man had dropped flat on his back in a drunken stupor, and had no suspicion of impending danger; the murderer had been able to choose his time, and select the position of the slash—at leisure.

Rollison shivered.

He saw a pair of suède shoes, badly needing cleaning, a crumpled yellow shirt, a collar but no tie; this man had lain down in his underclothes.

Was it "Pop?"

Who else could it be?

And—who had killed him?

Rollison went outside, leaving the room exactly as he had found it, and walked slowly down the stairs. Already possible implications were taking shape in his mind. Anxiety about the missing girl was changing to alarm for her, even though as yet there was no obvious need.

The street door was still closed. Rollison stepped to the window, peered out, and saw a policeman among the small crowd now gathered around the Bentley and the front door. Taking a card from his pocket, his name and address on one side, the monogram of the headless man on the other, he wrote across the *motifs:*

"You need the Murder Squad here, quickly. The b's upstairs." Then he went outside. The policeman, obviously on the alert for him, caught his eye. Rollison beckoned. Some of the stragglers moved away, but one or two, scenting a newer interest, drew closer.

"Everything all right, sir?" the constable asked.

"I can't complain," Rollison said. "Have a look at this, will you?" He handed over the card. The policeman looked down, and narrowed his eyes. If he asked questions in front of the crowd he would miss the chance which Rollison was giving him—of calling the Criminal Investigation Department before anyone else knew that the body had been discovered; they would have no idea what had happened even when the Murder Squad did arrive from the Division.

"I *see*, sir. Thank you." The man put the card in a breast pocket of his tunic. "You won't leave your car unattended for too long, will you? Souvenir hunters might get to work."

"I'll be off in a few minutes," Rollison promised. "You won't need me. When you do, you'll know where to find me."

"Thank you, sir." The man moved off without any show of haste.

Rollison went to the house next door, and knocked. The door opened almost at once, and a nice-looking boy stood there. He was eighteen or nineteen, as fair as Syd was dark.

"Are—are you Mr. Rollison?" he asked nervously. "The—Toff, I mean."

"Yes," said Rollison. "Is Syd Bishop——"

"He's just coming," the lad said. "I'm Jacky Henderson. Syd says Betty's had her baby. Is it all right? My Ma wants to know."

"Tell her the baby girl is fine," Rollison assured him. "Ma needn't worry."

Then Syd, bigger and broader and more manly by comparison appeared at Jacky's side.

"What's the hurry?" Syd demanded.

"I want to show you something," Rollison said. "Goodbye, Jacky." He took Bishop's wrist and led him back into his own house, pushing past the more boldly inquisitive neighbors. As he closed the door, he asked: "Did Ma Henderson notice anything?"

"Betty went out about twelve o'clock, that's all."

"Alone?"

"Yep."

"Was your father in?"

"He was at the pub—it was after opening hours, see." Bishop frowned into Rollison's face. "What's the matter?"

"Something you missed," Rollison said, simply to stall. He led the way upstairs and went ahead into the front bedroom, then turned in time to observe Syd Bishop's face when he saw the dead man.

Syd's cheeks blanched, and his eyes widened. He stood back, as Rollison had done, and Rollison felt almost convinced that sight of the body was as great a surprise to this young man as it had been to him.

But even if Syd had known what to expect, could he have steeled himself to show just this reaction?

Then the set lips moved, and the youth uttered a single hoarse word which sounded as if it had been forced out of his throat.

"*Pop!*" he groaned. "*Pop!*"

After a pause, Rollison said gently: "Syd, I've sent for the police. They'll be here in five minutes. Tell them everything, do you understand? Everything you can." There was no response and no reaction from the boy, even when Rollison went on: "Provided you didn't do this, I'll help you in every way I can."

51

Bishop just stared . . .

Rollison turned, went downstairs and out of the little house. A small boy scrambled out of the driving seat of the Bentley, and a woman hurrying up the road caught up with him and slapped his shaven head. Rollison took the wheel and drove off; as he reached the far corner he saw a police car turn in at the end of the road behind him.

Ten minutes later, he pulled up at a garage near Aldgate Station.

"I want to leave the car here for half an hour," he said to a pump attendant, slipped half a crown into an oily hand, and walked off.

Houndsditch was only a few minutes away.

He saw *Ticky's Gown and Mantle Manufacturers* on one side of the street, taking up the space of six or seven shops. On either side were fancy goods and leather goods wholesalers and warehouses with big window displays. Rollison remembered Grice once saying that a man named Osgood was under suspicion as the organizer of shop-lifting and bag-snatching; fancy goods were the easiest things to steal from shop counters. This seemed likely to be *his* Osgood.

The name of the firm stared blackly from green painted windows; it also hung in gold letters fastened by brackets to the smoke and smog-blackened brick wall. There seemed to be a hundred tiny windows at the second, third and fourth floors, and at each a woman was visible, head bent, shoulders bent as she worked.

A narrow door was marked: *Works Entrance*.

Rollison pushed this open to a small square hall, with a clock on one wall, and racks of time-cards alongside it. There was a notice-board, with half a dozen typewritten notes pinned to faded green baize—*Pop Night* read one; and Rollison pictured the old man.

Old? Only now did it register that "Pop" Bishop

52

couldn't have been more than fifty, might even be in his early forties.

A narrow concrete staircase with brick walls painted in high-gloss green paint led up to the first floor and a pair of double swing doors, marked: *Machinists*. As Rollison reached this door, it opened and a boy in black spectacles, with a mop of jet-black hair, came out.

He stopped short.

"Help you?" he inquired.

"Where do I find Mr. Osgood?"

"In there." The boy jerked his thumb over his shoulder.

Rollison pushed the double doors open, and stepped inside.

He expected that such an entry would attract attention, that anyone near the doors would look up. None did; *no one*. Yet there were a hundred people or more in the long narrow room which hummed with the ceaseless turning of electric motors, of needles stabbing up and down.

No one looked up; and no one stopped whatever work they were doing. There were a dozen men at big machines fastened to benches at one wall which was seventy or eighty feet long. Dozens of girls and women bent over sewing machines at other benches or tables which were at right angles to the long bench; these were about forty feet long, with a girl and machine every five feet. The women were all shapes, sizes and ages, some so old that they looked decrepit, some so young it looked as if they should be at school.

On a platform at the far end, obviously keeping an eye on every employee, was Osgood. Even from where Rollison stood, he looked outstandingly tall and bony. He was absorbed in some papers or a book, and did not look towards the door, although twice he glanced towards another part of the workroom. Fascinated, Rollison followed his gaze, and saw that in each case a girl had stopped working to make some adjustment to her machine. A streak of sunlight came in from one dim window, showing up the floating dust which must be everywhere in the room. Rollison could smell it, and already it began to irritate his nostrils.

He moved towards the platform. Now people glanced at him, almost furtively, but no one stopped what they were doing. He was within three yards of Osgood before the man looked in his direction. At first his eyes did not seem to focus. Then he recognised Rollison and reared back sharply, one hand in front of his chest as if in self-defence.

"Don't touch your gun," advised Rollison.

Behind him someone gasped.

Osgood gulped and from this angle Rollison saw the working of his prominent Adam's apple. He had a long, pointed nose, and not much chin. He wore a khaki-coloured smock, wide open at the neck, as was the spotless white shirt beneath it.

"Come on," said Rollison.

"What—what are you doing here?"

"I've come to get you."

"I'm not going anywhere."

"Oh yes, you are. You're coming with me."

"You—you've got a nerve!"

"Nerve enough to send for the police if you don't come quickly."

"*Police*," someone echoed, behind him.

"You—you've got nothing on me!"

"You're in for a big surprise," said Rollison. "Are you coming quietly or do I have to carry you?"

He was aware of other men moving from the bench towards him; they might be coming to attack him, or they might simply be curious. He realized that all the machines had stopped, and everyone was staring at him.

Osgood said shrilly: "Get him out of here!"

54

"Ossy," Rollison said very clearly, "you're coming with me. You're coming to see Syd Bishop—Betty's brother. You're going to tell him that you lied about me, and about Betty, and when he's finished with you, I'm going to make you take us to Betty. You'd better know where she is. Is that all clear?"

"You must be mad!"

"I'm getting mad," Rollison said. "I'm getting mean and mad. Come on."

"If you don't get out of here——"

Rollison jumped up on to the platform and Osgood sprang to his feet. He shot a glance of obvious appeal at the other men near Rollison, but none of them moved to help him. He made an ineffectual attempt to fend Rollison off, but was no more capable of doing so than he had been at the flat. Rollison grabbed his left wrist, twisted his arm round and then thrust him close to the table at which he had been working. Standing at one side, and a foot behind his captive, he saw the sea of pale faces and the stillness of everyone in the room.

He thrust Osgood's arm higher, until the man gasped in pain. One of the men in front of the table cleared his throat. It was Punchy Parks, whose slightly humped back was concealed by a grubby khaki-colored warehouse coat.

"What's the big idea?" he demanded shrilly.

"I want to make a little George Washington out of your friend Ossy."

"*Our* friend," exclaimed someone out of sight.

"Let him go," ordered Parks, but with little vehemence.

"Break the basket's arm!" a woman called out from the far end of the huge room.

Another woman giggled—a nervous sound which set off two or three others. A man said in a wondering tone:

"That's the Toff. You know, the *Toff!*"

55

"Why, he's in all the papers," a woman exclaimed, as if delighted. "Well, fancy seeing the Toff!"

"Make him let me go!" Osgood screeched.

He was still ahead of Rollison, his arm held high behind his back, taut enough to keep him motionless, but not enough to be really painful, although there was little doubt that he realised that if he jerked his arm he might break it. Rollison saw the sweat stealing down his cheek and dripping from his forehead, although it was not particularly hot in the room.

"What the hell's going on?" demanded Punchy Parks, the only man who attempted to intervene. "What are you trying to do, Rollison?"

"Break his bloody neck!" a woman called out.

"The foreman of the sweat shop doesn't seem popular with the labour force," Rollison remarked clearly. He raised his voice, startling everyone. "I want just one thing from Osgood," he declared. "Betty Bishop."

Someone asked: "Betty?"

"What's the matter with Betty?"

"Don't you see?" a third woman cried suddenly, "it was her baby at the Toff's flat. *Look!*"

She sprang up from her sewing machine, waving a newspaper, and immediately half a dozen others did the same, the rustle of papers replaced the whirr of the machines. Front page after front page was turned towards Rollison, and on everyone he saw his soubriquet in the headlines. On two were huge photographs of the child, on one the headline ran:

TOFF RESCUES NEWBORN BABE

Someone called in an anxious voice:

"What's this about Betty?"

"Hey, Mr. Rollison," said a man, "what do you know about this?"

"Is it *yours?*" demanded Punchy Parks. And now there was more power in his voice.

"According to your friend Ossy, yes," answered Rollison. "So Ossy told Syd Bishop, Betty's brother, and Syd came to break my neck. Ossy, why did you lie?" When the man simply stood still and helpless, the sweat still dripping down his cheeks, Rollison pushed his arm up a little higher. "Admit it—you lied to Syd Bishop."

"I didn't lie. She wouldn't have brought it to your place if it wasn't yours, would she? If anyone's lying, it's you." His defiance ended in a squeal: "Let me go, let me go!"

Rollison pushed the arm even higher, and silence fell upon the crowd, called by Osgood's sudden gasp.

"I'll deal with you for that later," Rollison said clearly. "Right now I want to know where Betty Bishop is." Osgood gasped, but said nothing more, and Rollison whispered into his ear: "Tell me if you know, or I'll let these women get at you. They don't seem to like you much."

Osgood maintained his stubborn silence.

After a moment's pause he raised his voice to the whole room. "Betty Bishop's missing. The baby found in my apartment was almost certainly hers, but she didn't take it there. I believe Osgood knows what happened to her. Why don't we make him talk?"

7

MOB

In the first few seconds following Rollison's question, there was a tense silence. He felt Osgood's body quivering; it seemed to cringe. Rollison sensed the antipathy of the workers to this man who so dominated them. The thought of using that antipathy to make Osgood talk had come swiftly, and he had lost no time taking advantage of it.

Now he wondered whether he had been wise, for on the faces of at least three women there were expressions which only one word could describe: hatred. He saw others also, sitting with tight lips and narrowed eyes, glaring at their helpless foreman.

One woman at the front called harshly: "Where's Betty?"

Another and another called: "Where is she?"

"Make him talk," yet another woman shouted. She picked up a pair of shining scissors, almost as large as a pair of shears, and moved towards Osgood. "*I'll* make him, if you want."

Osgood was muttering something which Rollison just caught:

"*I don't know. Tell them I don't know.*"

If he did know, surely he would say so under such pressure.

Punchy Parks said angrily: "Go back to your seat, Kate."

"Make him tell us where Betty is," the woman Kate insisted, and she took a step nearer. "*Come on, tell us.*"

"Tell us," screeched another woman.

"Tell us. Tell us!"

"Where's Betty Bishop?"

"Tell us, tell us, tell us!" It became a refrain, shrill, chanted in unison; and all the time the woman with the scissors drew nearer, as if she seriously intended to use the blades on Osgood if he did not speak.

He was cringing back and muttering:

"I swear it, I don't know, I swear it."

"Tell us, tell us, tell us, tell us!" The cry was louder still, and a note of menace had crept into the chanting. Other women were on their feet and beginning to advance. *"Tell us where Betty is. Tell us, tell us."*

Punchy gasped: "They'll tear him to pieces!"

That was easy for Rollison to believe.

What was more, and much, much worse, it was also easy for him to believe that he could not hold them back. There were at least a hundred of them, blocking the passages between the benches and the way to the door. The woman with the scissors was now only a few feet away, the blades pointing like a dagger towards Osgood's chest. Osgood was still muttering, but all the Toff could hear was a kind of gibberish, which might have been: *"I don't know, I swear it, I don't know."*

Parks said, anguished: "Put those down, Kate!"

Another man jumped on to the platform and muttered to Rollison:

"Now look what you've done."

Both men seemed convinced that the women would attack Osgood. There was some history of hatred here, of stored-up bitterness and resentment, and it had reached full flood, ugly and menacing. It was easy to believe that unless the foreman talked the women would attack him, and once an attack began there was no way of telling where it would end.

Then suddenly, the Toff put his ear close to Osgood's lips, flung up one hand and cried:

"He's told me!"

In that moment, and for the moment, the danger died away.

As the hush fell, Rollison saw the glitter in the eyes of the woman Kate, and guessed that there was something personal in her attitude, a malevolence which made her resentful that she could not use the scissors, or at least threaten Osgood with them to the point of terror. She was big, powerful-looking, deep-breasted, handsome in a gipsy-like way. Her gaze shifted from Osgood to Rollison as if she half suspected that he was lying.

She took a step nearer.

"Where's Betty?" she demanded. "Tell us all."

"It's enough for me to know," Rollison said sharply. The danger hadn't gone completely, for two or three other women crowded around Kate in physical as well as moral support.

"That's what *you* say." Kate's gaze on Rollison was now almost as hostile as it had been on Osgood. What could cause a hatred so great that a woman should seize such an opportunity as if it were a fortune?

Osgood was now limp against Rollison, who had loosened his hammer-lock. Punchy Parks, squaring his shoulders, went up to Kate, and spoke with a kind of authority he had not shown before.

"Get back to the machines, all of you."

"Who the hell are you trying to order about?" Kate flashed at him.

Punchy moistened his lips.

"You *and* all the others," he said, his boldness touched by fear of the woman who towered over him. "I'm in charge when Mr. Osgood's not here. We've lost half an hour's production already, and that won't do your pay-packets any good." He stood squarely up to the woman with a defiance which Rollison silently applauded.

A woman at the back said half-heartedly: "Better get started."

"Why don't we take the day off?" demanded a blonde with a face like a newborn chick's.

"As soon as I've found Betty Bishop, I'll send word,"

promised Rollison. He forced a laugh which he didn't feel, but there was deep relief in him. "Then follow the breathless adventures of the Toff in the *Daily Mirror*, *Sketch*, *Sun*——" He streamed the names out one after another, and soon half the workpeople were laughing. But not Kate; she stared at him with bold defiance, as if she were simply biding her time.

Rollison suddenly shifted his position, made a back and hoisted Osgood on to it. He carried the unprotesting man over his shoulder like a sack of potatoes, and stepped down from the platform. The laughter was still good-natured, although there was a note of derision in much of it.

"Clear the way," Rollison ordered.

"Put him down!" cried Parks. "You'll injure him."

Rollison moved towards the door, and now only Kate stood in his path. He did not slacken his pace.

Kate still stared at him with hostility, but the defiance, the bravado, seemed to be giving way to resentment. Her eyes followed him sullenly. "You didn't fool me."

Rollison flashed her a smile which had been known to melt hearts supposed to be of stone.

"Only a fool would try," he said.

Next moment, he was past her. A boy held the double doors wide open, and he strode out. Osgood's feet bumped against his thighs. No one was at the foot of the stairs, but passers-by stared as he strode into the street, carrying his burden. A barrow-boy loading oranges put his head on one side and asked:

"Want any help, Guv'ner?"

"You could get me a taxi."

"Ambulance, more like it."

Two or three people laughed.

A taxi came along with its sign lighted, and pulled in. Rollison thrust Osgood into it, watched by at least a dozen people. No one made any attempt to stop him, and no one showed any untoward curiosity.

"Where to, sir?"

"The Blue Dog, off Mile End Road."

"Right you are."

Ten minutes later they pulled up outside the old, red-brick public house, which was one of the features of the East End of London. Not only did the inn sign depict a bull-dog colored bright blue but the woodwork was painted the same colour, almost dazzling against the dull red brick. Beyond the pub, which stood at a corner, was a large wooden structure with a signboard over the front door reading: EBUTT'S GYMNASIUM. This, like the Blue Dog, was owned by Bill Ebbutt, an old and trusted friend of the Toff.

A seedy-looking individual in cap and muffler stood at the door, watching the taxi as if with casual interest. As Rollison appeared, this man was galvanized into action. His face stretched as if it were made of india rubber, his neck seemed to double in length, ostrichlike. Here he was known baldly as "Rube," but whether it was his baptismal, or his family, name, or merely a sobriquet, nobody had troubled to find out. Now, putting his head inside the building, he called:

"It's the blinking Torf!"

Then he sprang towards Rollison, who was pulling Osgood out of the taxi, feet first.

"Let me," he urged, and took one leg and pulled.

"Mind his head!" cried Rollison.

Osgood's head bumped on the floor of the cab, and the rubbery-faced man, trying to save it from a further crack, actually banged it again. Rollison helped to get Osgood on his feet. He was obviously semi-conscious, a fact which puzzled Rollison, who had first suspected that he was putting on an act; had the two bumps put him out?

"Mr. Ar!" A big man of enormous girth came bustling out of the gymnasium. He had three chins, small, almost delicate features set in a pale and flabby face, and wore a polo-necked seaman's sweater, stretched so that the white of his under-vest showed like a pattern between the stitches. Two others, smaller and younger men, followed him and came at the double towards Rollison.

They took Osgood between them.

"What do you want doing with him?" inquired Ebbutt, as if he were talking of a stuffed animal.

"Put him in a camp-bed and try to bring him round," said Rollison.

"What's up with him?"

"Try to find that out, too," Rollison pleaded.

"You heard Mr. Ar," Ebbutt said to the others. "Get cracking." He reached Rollison, stretched out a big, bruised hand on which the swollen knuckles stood out like misshapen new potatoes, gripped Rollison's hand and took his arm. "Good to see you, Mr. Ar, but I don't much like the company you keep."

"So you know Osgood?"

"I know him only too well. He's fixed more fights than anyone in London. Warned him out of my place a dozen times, I have. Take it from me, Mr. Ar, he's no good. Hasn't got an honest thought in his head, and never done a decent thing in his life." They entered the big gymnasium together, Ebbutt talking earnestly as they passed the wall bars, vaulting horses, parallel bars, punch-balls, and walked between two rings, the ropes of one tightened ready for a match.

Osgood was already stretched out on a camp-bed in a corner, Rube standing at the head as a small man in a detergent-white sweater came in and bent over him, taking his right wrist.

"So he's a congenital liar, thief and general no-good," Rollison said, looking down at Osgood, whose feet overlapped the end of the bed.

"You've said it. *And* more."

"More?" inquired Rollison, interestedly.

"Never been able to understand it," said Ebbutt, genuinely marveling, "but women fall for him. Can *you* see what appeals to them? Proper Don Juan, he is—got little bastards spread all over London. There must be more husbands who would like to stick a knife in Osgood's back than you can count. I will say one thing for him, though."

Osgood was turning his head from side to side, as if in pain, and his eyes were flickering open.

"That ought to be fascinating," said Rollison. "What's good about him?"

"He's no fool, *and* he can talk himself out of anything."

"Say that again," said Rube. "I gotta make a call," he added, and went out.

"Something must have put Osgood off his stroke today," Rollison remarked drily.

"You're enough to put anyone off his stroke." Ebbutt was seized by a fit of laughing which turned into an asthmatic cough.

Rollison took the opportunity to begin telling his story, and Ebbutt and the others listened intently. When it was over, all of them were staring at Osgood, whose eyes were now half open, while the man in the white sweater also stood looking down at him, obviously puzzled. He was Gabby Gay, the official trainer, first aid man and masseur.

"Now what I think," he paused.

"Well, what do you think?" Ebbutt grumbled.

"He's out for a long time," stated Gabby.

"Concussion, you mean?"

"Seems like it to me."

"Could it be an act?" asked Rollison.

"Sure, it *could* be, but I don't think it is."

"If he's putting on an act I'll soon find out," said Ebbutt. "Put him under the cold shower first, then the hot one. Surprising how soon that gets rid of some kinds of concussion."

"If you ask me," said Gabby, seriously, "he ought to see a doctor."

"Now don't make a big deal out of it," protested Ebbutt.

"Well, you asked me, and I've told you what I think," said Gabby. He rubbed his hands together, like a cymbal player, making a slithery noise. "I wash my hands of him. Okay?"

As Rollison studied the sharp, bird-like features of the man on the bed, Ebbutt asked in a wheezier voice than ever:

"What do you want me to do, Mr. Ar? Apart from bringing this so-and-so round, I mean." When Rollison didn't answer, Ebbutt went on: "You could have looked after Osgood anywhere, you didn't have to bring him here. So what's on your mind?"

Rollison smiled, with sudden warmth.

"Always on the ball, Bill. Thanks. I want to know where Betty Bishop is. The police may find her, but if she's in hiding, your chaps are much more likely to hear where. As soon as you know, tell me."

"Okay. And the rest?"

"There's a man named Parks, a friend of Osgood——"

"I know Punchy Parks."

"Find him, and try to find out what he knows—if someone put Osgood up to naming me; why he and Osgood came to my flat; whether they brought the baby there, and if they didn't, who did?"

"I get the angle," Ebbutt declared. "I'll see what I can do, Mr. Ar. How about having a man to stand-in for Jolly? Percy Wrightson's away, but I could send someone."

"I'll let you know," Rollison answered. He saw difficulties ahead with an Ebbutt man if Perdita stayed at the flat, hence his caution. That was the first time he had thought of Perdita since he had straddled the pillion of Syd Bishop's motor-cycle. A mental picture of her let in a stream of thoughts about everything that had happened since he had left Gresham Terrace.

He had even forgotten the cold-blooded murder of Syd Bishop's father, but now he had a swift picture of the man's face, and another of Syd Bishop's, with those fine dark eyes and sweeping lashes. He was still picturing the youth, when Rube appeared at the door and called shrilly:

"The cops are coming! You want to make yourself scarce, Mr. Ar?"

8

SUPERINTENDENT GRICE

Rollison, far from wanting to make himself scarce, stepped outside the gymnasium to see the police car. The man who was getting out surprised him, for it was Superintendent William Grice of New Scotland Yard. Usually Divisional men operated here; there must be some significant reason for one of the Yard's chiefs coming. Grice was a tall, well-groomed man, good-looking in a rather severe way. His brown hair was streaked with gray, and on one side of his face was an ugly scar, memento of a wound caused when a parcel bomb had blown up in his face.

The bomb had been intended for the Toff.

From that time on there had been a bond between them, respect and understanding deepening over the years into friendship. Now and again the very nature of the cases which Rollison investigated and the methods he used, caused a conflict of interests between them, but this was seldom acute and rarely lasted long.

Now Grice was smiling rather tensely. No one else was with him, except the driver, who stood by the open door of the car.

"Hallo, Bill," Rollison welcomed.

"Hallo," Grice said. His handshake was almost perfunctory. "I'd like a quiet word with you."

"How about using my office?" suggested Ebbutt, eagerly. "Plenty of room there."

In fact, it was a box of an office, with room only for two contemporary chairs, their legs like spikes, their seats and backs of thick sponge rubber. Both men sank into these, adjusting their feet punctiliously so that they did not kick each other. Ebbutt shut the door firmly.

"Well?" Rollison asked.

"Three things," said Grice, abruptly. "First, this baby story."

"The papers have everything right except the implications," Rollison told him. "Have you found the mother yet?"

"No, but we're doing all we can. Did Mario Bishop bring the baby to you?"

Rollison said, startled: "Do you mean Syd's father?"

"Yes."

"Not as far as I know, but in any case I don't know who it was."

Grice's eyes had a piercing, almost accusing expression. "Sure?"

"Positive."

"I never know whether to believe you or not," Grice said, a little querulously. "What's it all about?"

"I don't know that either."

Grice said heavily: "Do you seriously mean this whole business started last night when they dumped the baby on your doorstep?"

"That's when it started as far as I'm concerned."

"Then why go to Ticky's this morning? Why attack Osgood?" When Rollison kept silence, Grice went on: "We had a complaint about you at the Yard—charging you with assault on Osgood, alarming the whole staff, damaging some machines—and abduction. Where is Osgood now?"

"Not ten yards away from you," Rollison answered.

Grice started, and turned his head.

"Here?"

"Ebbutt's trainer thinks he needs a doctor."

"*I sent for one, Mr. Ar!*" boomed Ebbutt. Thus at one and the same moment he proved that he was close to the wooden wall and could hear every word—and that he did not give a damn who knew it. "Should be here in two shakes of a lamb's tail!"

68

"Rolly," Grice said, "why did you bring Osgood here?"

"Because I think he may know where Betty Bishop is," answered Rollison. "I softened him up and hoped he would tell me when we got here, but on the way he either put on an act, or went sick on me."

"Have you hurt him?"

"I manhandled him a little, but not enough to hurt a fly."

"That's not what we were told. Someone telephoned to say you subjected him to a brutal attack."

"Well, it shouldn't be hard to prove," Rollison said, feeling a little sore. "There were over a hundred women present. Who lodged the complaint?"

"A woman."

"Name?"

"She didn't give one."

"What's happening at the Yard, Bill? Since when did you start taking action on the strength of an anonymous phone call?"

"We're interested in Osgood," Grice announced.

"What's he been up to?" Rollison asked, wondering if the shop-lifting crimes could now be proved against the man.

"Everything under the sun!" Grice would never know how much like Ebbutt he sounded when he said that. "In this particular case we have reason to believe he organizes a lot of bag-snatching, shop-lifting and housebreaking."

"You just believe?"

"We know, and we don't need much more to make it a hard-and-fast case," Grice amended. "We believe he sells a lot of the stolen goods in nearby warehouses and in Petticoat Lane. If he doesn't, somebody does. Come clean, Rolly. You're on to the same business."

"Cross my heart, I'd never heard of it," Rollison said, and echoed: "He organizes bag-snatching, shop-lifting and housebreaking, and sells the proceeds through the

Houndsditch area wholesalers, and in the Lane. I'm trying to see how this would fit in with what little I know."

"What little do you know?"

"I think he tried to frame me for . . ." began Rollison, and went into as much detail as he considered necessary. Grice relaxed enough to smile, as if the false charge of fatherhood had its amusing side. When Rollison finished Grice shifted back in his chair, and stood up. As he moved towards the door, he said almost casually:

"Where does Mrs. Shortt come into this?"

"Perdita?" Rollison asked in surprise. "What on earth makes you think she comes into it anywhere?"

"That sticks out a mile."

"You couldn't be more wrong."

"Nonsense!" protested Grice, brusquely. "Here's a woman whom you take to your flat, and who's obviously well-equipped to look after that baby. Afterwards, she keeps telephoning the hospital—she's been in touch with them four times this morning. Do you think that's just out of goodness of heart?"

The question jolted Rollison badly.

He was still deeply preoccupied by its implication when Grice left him to see Osgood. The doctor was examining the man, but could find nothing worse with him than a state of shock.

This implication was nonsense, of course; it had to be nonsense. He, Rollison, had been introduced to Perdita only the night before, it was sheer coincidence that she had been at his flat on the night that the baby had been abandoned, coincidence that she had been able to cope so well. There was not the slightest reason for thinking that Perdita might have arranged the introduction, might have planned to be with him on this particular night. And yet—he *had* been surprised that she had come to the flat with him.

Could she have schemed the visit?

But even if she had, how could she possibly have had foreknowledge of the foundling? Dammit, the child hadn't been born many hours before it had been discovered. Certainly Perdita could not have planned to show her skill as a nurse on the night when she and Rollison had met.

Grice was being absurd; and yet he had put a sliver of doubt into Rollison's mind.

Now Grice said: "What do you intend to do with Osgood?"

"I'd hoped to engage him in a little light-hearted conversation," Rollison said brightly, "but I don't suppose it's any good now. Do you know where he lives?"

"*I* do," Gabby the trainer piped up.

"Better take him home, then," put in the doctor. "Anything more you want me for, Bill?" He meant Ebbutt.

"Not unless Mr. Grice——"

"No, thanks," said Grice. Only when the doctor and Gabby had gone, and two others were helping Osgood unsteadily to his feet, did he ask Rollison: "Have you any idea what might have put him out like this?"

"Nothing that happened at Ticky's. He banged his head on the cab step once."

Grice gave Rollison a speculative look, pursed his lips, and said:

"That doesn't square with the anonymous complaint."

"One hundred women witnesses can't be wrong," Rollison said lightly. That was the one aspect of the situation about which he had no qualms at all.

"Can I give you a lift?" asked Grice, resignedly.

"If you'd take me to Aldgate, I'd be grateful," Rollison said, and got into the back of Grice's car. Once they started off, watched by Bill Ebbutt and Rube, the driver began to report on information which had come over the air while his chief had been in the gymnasium. Rollison listened with half an ear only; his chief preoccupation was still with Perdita Shortt and Grice's innuendo.

71

". . . taken to Divisional Police Headquarters where he is being questioned concerning the murder of his father. In Richmond——"

"Who was that?" asked Rollison sharply.

"Didn't you hear?" asked Grice. "That was about young Bishop."

"Is *he* a suspect?"

"Don't you suspect him?" demanded Grice.

"That boy? I do not!"

"What's the matter with you in this affair?" demanded Grice. "You aren't seeing the obvious. You're being taken for a ride, and you'd better watch out."

"I'll begin now," said Rollison with mock humbleness.

"There's another thing I'd like you to begin," Grice said. "A full and detailed statement of everything that's happened to you, or you've done, since that baby was put on your doorstep."

"Threshold," corrected Rollison. "Okay, I'll do that, Bill. Drop me here, driver, will you?"

He nodded to Grice as he got out of the police car near the garage where he had left the Bentley. It was waiting regally, windscreen washed and chromium glistening. As he opened the car door, he saw a fold of paper on the seat. His bill? The petrol attendant came up.

"Fill her up, sir?"

"Please." Rollison opened the note, and stared down at two words pencilled in black capital letters. The tension in his manner must have revealed itself, for the attendant stared at him wonderingly.

The two words were: "HI, POP!"

All that Rollison could learn from the garage hand was that several girls from the factories near by, as well as several youths and a group of schoolboys, had gathered round the car admiringly. He could not remember anyone opening the door, but part of the time he had been at the pumps, with his back to the Bentley.

Rollison smiled broadly, so that anyone watching

72

would have no reason to believe that he took the note seriously, got into the driving seat and drove away. As he turned into the main road, a group of factory girls waiting at a corner saw him. The woman Kate, among them, shook her fist, and others followed suit. It passed through Rollison's mind that they might resent the fact that he had taken their foreman out of their clutches. Then he wondered why they had such animosity towards Osgood. Through the narrow streets of the city of London he had to crawl in line with buses and trucks and taxis and private cars, but once past the Bank of England he was able to drive more freely. High Holborn ran into Oxford Street, and Oxford Street led to Marble Arch; soon he was in Park Lane, turning left, right and left again, and at last he reached Gresham Terrace.

Outside Number 22 was a small crowd, including two men with cameras, and on the roof of an ITV News van was a man at the back of a television camera. Suddenly there was a cry: "Here he is!"

The television camera swiveled round and started whirring, men came hurrying up as Rollison slowed down. Two policemen cleared a path for him. He drew up and double-parked, no unusual thing in Gresham Terrace. As he got out, a wag at the back of the crowd shouted:

"Hi, Pop!"

Rollison smiled brightly and waved into the cameras, then went inside the street door of Number 22, where he found four newspapermen on the stairs with more questions about Perdita, the baby and the Bishops. He did not know whether Perdita was in the flat, and after flinging casual, carefree answers to the loaded questions of the newspapermen, he took out his key, remembering vividly just how he had taken it out the previous night.

Before he could put it into the lock, the door opened, and Jolly, his man, stood there.

"Good morning, sir," said Jolly. "I trust I find you well."

9

ADVICE FROM JOLLY

Jolly was in his early sixties, and looked as if he had once been fat and was now thin; he had, in fact, never been fat, but had acquired lines and a rather bulgy jowl by the simple passing of years. He had the heavily shadowed, melancholy brown eyes usually associated with spaniels, which, with his other characteristics, combined to give him a slightly dyspeptic and somewhat pessimistic appearance.

"Jolly," said Rollison fervently, "I've never been so glad to see you." He shook Jolly's hand as they went into the lounge hall, Jolly closing the door firmly on the clicking cameras and babel of voices behind them. "Are we alone?"

"Yes, sir."

"I don't know whether to be glad or sorry. You would never believe——"

"What I read in the newspapers, sir?"

"So that's what's brought you."

"That, aided by the fact that my brother is much improved," said Jolly. "I imagine that the material details of the report are accurate."

They reached the living-room.

"Yes," Rollison answered, looking about quickly. On the Trophy Wall, which took up the whole of the space behind his desk, was an envelope addressed in clear, neat handwriting to THE TOFF. He went towards it eagerly, guessing who it was from, guessing that Jolly had noticed it and deliberately left it in full sight.

It was resting on the box of poisoned chocolates he had shown Perdita.

"Lunch?" he inquired.

"In fifteen minutes, sir."

"Bring yours in too, and I'll tell you all about everything," promised Rollison.

He sat at his desk and slit the envelope open with a paperknife which had a handle of New Zealand pauna-shell. He drew out a sheet of his own letter-heading, unfolded it, and read:

> Hi, Pop!
>   I'm going to the hospital to see our infant, and then to my flat. May I come and see you about three-thirty?
>
> > Daringly,
> > > Perdita.

Rollison actually chuckled.

Then a spasm almost of pain caught him, and he drew out his wallet, and then the note which he had found on the seat of his car. There was not the faintest similarity in the lettering—what a fool, of course there wasn't!—and the phrase was one which would spring to the mind of anyone who wanted to tease, or take a rise out of him.

Why would Perdita want to do that, except out of natural exuberance?

Why was she so intensely interested in the baby? Simply out of natural warm-heartedness?

Why had Grice made it so obvious that he, Rollison, ought to think seriously about Perdita, and her possible motives for getting to know him?

If these personal preoccupations weren't enough, there was anxiety for Betty Bishop, but at least the Yard was on the look out for her. He felt a new kind of anxiety for Syd Bishop, too. What was it Grice had said when he had scoffed at the idea of Syd having murdered his own father?

75

"What's the matter with you in this affair?" Grice had demanded. "You aren't seeing the obvious. You're being taken for a ride, and you'd better watch out."

Rollison was sitting contemplating these words, acknowledging that Grice had been wholly serious, when the telephone bell rang. He shifted his position so as to answer it. On the desk was the typewritten statement he had made to Police Sergeant Wills the previous night.

"Richard Rollison," he said.

"Mr. Wiseman of the *Daily Globe* would like to speak to you please, sir." There was a pause during which Rollison skimmed through the statement, a click or two. Finally Wiseman came on the line, speaking in the high voice which was always liable to sound impatient.

"Rolly?"

"Hallo, Mick."

"What's this about you attacking a man named Osgood?"

"I hardly laid a finger on him," Rollison protested.

"Oh, come. You can't get away with that one."

"I've already told the Yard, there were a hundred witnesses."

"Of the way you beat Osgood up," Wiseman asserted.

"Oh, don't be a bloody fool!"

"It's no use losing your temper." Wiseman's voice rose almost to falsetto. "I had two men and a photographer at Ticky's—they've just come back. They talked to a dozen of the seamstresses and machinists, and every statement was the same. What made you get so violent with Osgood?"

Rollison did not answer, but stared down at Perdita's note with its "Hi, Pop!" and the penciled words on the other slip of paper. He almost forgot that Wiseman was still on the line.

"You heard me?" Wiseman asked, with an annoyed, accusing note in his voice.

"Er—yes. Yes, I heard you," admitted Rollison. "I'm

beginning to realize that both you and the police have reason to believe something which isn't true. I didn't beat Osgood up—not in the way you've been led to believe—and the witnesses were not hostile to me at the time."

"Well, they are now!"

"So I gather. Mick, will you do something for me?"

"If it's legal," Wiseman said almost grudgingly. "What is it?"

"Will you get the names and addresses of the people who saw me at Ticky's this morning—as many as you can. I may want to talk to some of them."

"Anyone in particular?"

"Yes. A big, handsome woman named Kate."

"Kate McGuire," Wiseman stated, without hesitation. "She was the one who telephoned us and said it was worth sending a reporter and photographer. I don't know her address, but I can find out." After a pause, Wiseman went on: "Why are you so interested in her?"

Rollison answered vaguely:

"Oh, well. A very handsome woman, isn't she? I'll be particularly grateful for her address. Were you going to say something else?"

Wiseman asked, quite seriously:

"Are you feeling all right, Rolly?"

"A bit baffled, otherwise I'm fine."

"I mean—*you* weren't hurt, were you?"

"Concussed, you mean," suggested Rollison. "Punch drunk? Knocked so silly that I forget what really happened, even forget the way I'm supposed to have gone berserk at Ticky's. I don't think so, Mick. I'll ask Jolly. Bye."

He rang off.

After a few seconds, he began to feel calm enough to smile, ruminatively, although this new slant was no laughing matter. *Was* it possible that Grice was right and that he was really being taken for a ride?

If so—why?

He pondered as he finished skimming the statement, and signed it. Soon, Jolly's voice, pitched on a low, considerate key, interrupted these thoughts.

"Lunch is ready, sir."

"Ah! Yes. Thanks." Rollison sprang up. "Jolly, we have a thousand preoccupations, and we need a cool, calm, objective mind like yours to put them in their proper perspective. When I've told you everything I shall expect you to contemplate and consider, and be ready with all the answers by three-fifteen."

"Why three-fifteen, sir?" Jolly glanced up at the clock over the mantelpiece; it was nearly half past one.

"Mrs. Shortt will be here at three-thirty."

"Indeed, sir?"

"Of course, you don't know Mrs. Shortt," Rollison said. "I really will have to start from the beginning, won't I?" He sat down to salmon, wafer-thin brown bread and butter, and segments of lemon; sprinkling red pepper over this, he began to eat and talk. Jolly ate and listened, getting up periodically to bring in minute steaks, pan-fried potatoes, new peas and new carrots, followed by Cheshire cheese, crackers and farmhouse butter. They took coffee into the big room, Rollison still narrating.

He stopped at five minutes to three.

"You've got twenty minutes to come up with all the answers," he declared.

Jolly, sitting back in an easy chair, was more friend and counsellor than servant. He pursed his lips, studied Rollison's face and said almost primly:

"I don't think I shall require tewnty minutes, sir."

Rollison was startled.

"You find it that simple?"

"One aspect of it, beyond all need for reflection."

"Show me," pleaded Rollison.

"There can be no doubt at all that you are the victim of a premeditated campaign to embarrass and discredit you," Jolly said. "Clearly, there were indications that a paternity suit might be brought against you. As clearly, there is a form of blackmail being used against you—particularly this *volte-face* on the part of the workers at this place—ah—Ticky's." The way he said "Ticky's" was icily supercilious. "If the man Osgood is in fact feigning illness, that is yet another form of blackmail. If I may say so, sir, there are three matters which need our urgent attention."

"Name them," urged Rollison.

"First—we must ascertain whether Osgood is suffering from a genuine illness; or one induced by a drug; or whether he is feigning his present condition. Shall I see to that?"

"Yes."

"Second—we must discover what influence could be brought to bear on the women as well as the men at—ah —Ticky's, to change their attitude so quickly. There is no doubt in your mind that they were both dominated by and yet seriously antagonistic towards Osgood, is there?"

"None. Could be cause and effect."

"No doubt, sir. However some pressure must have been brought to bear after you had gone, to re-establish the domination over them."

"I'd thought of that," said Rollison. "I'm getting some addresses from Wiseman, remember."

"I do indeed, but I doubt whether you can handle the inquiry personally, sir. I think that some of Ebbutt's men, working on different employees of Ticky's, would be most likely to find out what caused the change."

"Jolly."

"Sir?"

"Blackmail or bribery, obviously."

"Indeed yes, sir. But which?"

"In this case, blackmail."

"Why do you feel so sure?"

"You can blackmail a crowd by using the threat of dismissal, for instance, or by the victimization of isolated individuals. But greed is not so universal as fear, and you can't *bribe* a crowd. There will always be one or two with a conscience or a keen sense of independence."

"I think that may be so," conceded Jolly, "but it is by no means certain. Shall I instigate that line of inquiry?"

"Leave something for me to do," pleaded Rollison.

"Indeed I will, sir—the most important contribution, as I see it."

"Mrs. Shortt?" said Rollison, almost eagerly.

"No, sir, not at all. Sydney Bishop, and his sister. This will be particularly vital if Sydney Bishop is detained and charged. It is the kind of investigation for which you are most renowned. As a matter of fact, I wonder——" Jolly hesitated, but Rollison did not prompt him. "I wonder whether the affair at Ticky's could possibly be an effort to prevent you from watching the young man's interests."

Rollison did not comment.

"I understand that you discovered the body of the father, sent for the police in a most discreet way and went straight from there to Ticky's. It is conceivable that the young man, Sydney, was to be framed for the murder, and obviously your intervention could prevent this."

"I don't see it," Rollison objected.

"What is it that escapes you, sir?"

"Why anyone started to implicate me, by bringing the baby to the flat. Whether the same people followed this up by sending round young Bishop, convincing him that I'd been playing fast and loose with his sister. Whether there is some Mr. Big who checked the result of this by sending Osgood and Parks here. I would say all that was done before Bishop was murdered, and so his son couldn't have been framed before the event—the suspicion falls on him by sheer chance."

"I don't think you are seeing the matter clearly, sir," Jolly said. A momentary change of expression suggested that he wished he could bite back the words as soon as they were uttered, but Grice had said virtually the same thing. Rollison studied Jolly carefully.

"Show me the real picture," he invited at last.

"Much of this could have been arranged to lure you to Gill Street," Jolly answered, choosing his words with great precision. "The placing of the child, the visit from Osgood to draw your attention to him, the visit from Sydney Bishop, to make it likely you would take an interest in him—I think it probable that all of these moves were planned well in advance, sir."

"I see," Rollison said. "Why should Osgood or anyone wish to draw my attention to him?"

"Is there any point in guessing?"

"Tell me what's on your mind."

"Osgood did come, without disguise, making it virtually certain that you would recognize him again."

"I could have been fooled into thinking he was a man from the *Globe*."

"Did his behavior really make that likely, sir?"

After a pause, Rollison said: "No, I suppose not. So by your reasoning Osgood came to find out something he badly wanted to know. And he started to search the flat. I wonder why?" he added softly.

"As I said, sir, there seems little point in guessing." Jolly's tone was almost disapproving now.

"If he didn't know where Betty was, he might have wondered if she was at the flat," Rollison went on. Before Jolly—slightly more impressed by this suggestion—could comment, however, there was a ring at the front door bell. Rollison glanced at his watch and saw it was exactly three-thirty. He felt instantly more cheerful, and also realized how much he had been looking forward to seeing Perdita. Jolly went out of the room, inclining his head as he went, and Rollison moved to the chair behind the desk, but did not sit down.

Was it Perdita?

One syllable told him that it was. "Oh!" ejaculated Perdita, and over Jolly's: "Good afternoon, Madam," she went on: "You must be Jolly. Is Mr. Rollison in?" She sounded brisk.

"Yes, Madam, he is expecting you."

Rollison heard Perdita's hurried footsteps, and rose to welcome her with a smile. But she was not smiling at him, she was glaring; it was obvious that she was very angry. Her eyes flashed and her lips were parted and she looked breathtakingly beautiful.

10

PERDITA'S ANGER

"You!" Perdita cried furiously. "You ought to be horse-whipped!"

Rollison was so startled that he could find no reply.

"Don't stand there grinning like a satyr. You ought to be horse-whipped!"

Jolly was at the door, looking almost apprehensive.

Rollison moved forward.

"You sound like a Victorian papa," he protested.

"If I were a Victorian papa I *would* horse-whip you." Perdita's gaze turned stormily towards the Trophy Wall, as if she were looking for a weapon. "Of all the deceitful, treacherous *pigs*, you're the nastiest I've ever met."

"Perdita, what on earth——"

"Don't talk to me!"

"Perdita, please——"

"I hope I *never* see you again."

His first surprise over, Rollison was now getting his second wind.

"Perdita," he said, "for goodness sake grow up."

Still standing in the doorway, Jolly smiled more hopefully.

"*What* did you say?" demanded Perdita.

"I told you to grow up," repeated Rollison firmly. "You're behaving like a schoolgirl and it doesn't suit you."

"Why——!" Perdita stepped forward, eyes flashing even more furiously than before.

Rollison rounded the desk purposefully and she turned to face him. Anger still flared in her eyes, but now there was alarm, too. Sliding his arms about her shoulders, he pulled her towards him, and, as she struggled to free herself, lifted a hand to the back of her head and pressed his lips against hers. At first he was uncomfortably aware of Jolly, who was gazing blandly at the scene before turning slowly away. Then he forgot everything except Perdita. But her body remained stiff and unyielding against his own, her lips were unresponsive, and when at last he let her go he wondered whether he had made a mistake.

"You are a beast," she said coldly.

"You are behaving like a silly little girl," Rollison retorted.

"*What?*"

"A silly, *forgetful*, little girl."

"I don't know what you're talking about."

"Don't you remember saying that we must always be honest with each other?"

After a pause, she echoed, "*Honest?*" After another pause, she added, "Yes, I *do* remember." Her expression softened a little; so did her tone of voice, but there was still an edge to it. "You really mean I'm behaving badly?"

"I really mean you're behaving like a spoilt child."

Perdita gave a strangled laugh. "If that's what *I* am, then what are you?"

"A satyr who ought to be horse-whipped; but who doesn't know why."

"You do know why," Perdita said with feeling. "You know perfectly well why."

"Perdita," said Rollison, trying to preserve this new and welcome calm, "has someone convinced you that I *am* the villain of this piece? That I *am* that child's father?"

Perdita looked startled.

"No, no, of course not." She paused. Then the words came out with a rush. "But you gave my name to the newspapers and it's all over London, *and* my photograph, *and* you told them that I spent the night here. It's unforgivable."

84

Slowly, Rollison said: "It certainly would be, if I had done so." He did not remind her that he had warned her that unpleasant publicity might come of her recklessness.

"Then why did you do it?"

"Perdita," Rollison said gently, "don't be silly."

It was probably as much the expression on his face as his tone of voice which affected her, and Rollison noticed that at last she began to look calmer.

"*Didn't* you do it?"

"You ought to be spanked for believing I did."

A glimmer of a smile showed in her eyes.

"Not horse-whipped?"

Rollison gripped her hands for a moment, then released her, and went back to the other side of the desk.

"Who told you I'd told the Press?"

"A man at the hospital."

"That young doctor?"

"Well——" Perdita began to color slightly.

"Did he?"

"He asked some newspapermen who were there, and they said they had it from you—oh, I was so angry."

"I should be, not you," Rollison said. "When the doctor reported it to the police, there was no way of keeping it from the newspapers, but I certainly didn't give anyone any details. Did you seriously believe I did? Had you forgotten you talked to the Press yourself?"

In a moment Perdita was all contrition.

"Rolly, I had, I really had! I'm so sorry."

"Prove it by staying here another night and finding out whether that's in the newspapers, too." They laughed together, and with their laughter, the whole mood changed. "Seriously," went on Rollison, "how's the child?"

"Still in an incubator, but they say she's doing fine."

"Good. Have you been home?"

"Yes, but only to have a snack and see if there was any

mail. Just bills," she added with a grimace. "Rolly, what's all this about you attacking a man in some factory?"

Rollison began to explain, and in doing so was vividly reminded of the *volte-face* of the women workers at Ticky's. But before he was able to finish, the telephone bell rang. He could leave the call for Jolly to take on the extension, but for some reason he wanted a respite from telling the story, so he picked up the receiver. At once he heard the conspiratorial tones of Bill Ebbutt.

"Mr. Rollison?"

"Here I am, Bill."

"Mr. Ar?" Ebbutt's voice rose. "Mr. Ar, there's that woman named Kate McGuire you was asking about."

"Yes, Bill."

"She's got a house in Camberwell, 93 Circle Road," Ebbutt declared.

"Thanks, Bill," said Rollison warmly. "I'll pay her a call."

"You be careful," warned Ebbutt. "I can tell you another thing."

"Go on."

"Betty Bishop used to go to this McGuire woman's place reg'lar," Ebbutt told him. "It's a kind of an apartment house. Flatlets. A lot of single women live there. That what you wanted to know?"

"It's one thing," Rollison said softly. "It is indeed. Hold on, Bill, I think Jolly wants a word with you——"

Jolly had a word or more with Bill Ebbutt, while Rollison finished what he was saying to Perdita. It was obvious that he was not giving her his undivided attention, but she did not complain. Nor did she protest when Rollison told her that he must go out.

"Rolly," she said, as he moved away from her, "be very careful."

"I'll be so careful you wouldn't recognize me," he promised.

As he told Jolly where he was going, as he went downstairs, as he took the wheel of the Bentley, he found himself thinking about Perdita more than about Kate McGuire. Why had she urged him to be careful? Why had she really arrived in such a temper? Could Grice possibly be right in thinking that she was worth considering as a suspect? For that matter, had Grice really implied as much as that or had he, Rollison, only inferred it?

He drove this time to his own garage, left the Bentley and took a taxi to Camberwell. As it crossed Lambeth Bridge, a strong and gusty wind swept along the river, whipping up the surface, which looked steely gray and cold. No one showed any interest in Rollison, who paid the cab off at the end of Circle Road, then strolled along it.

He passed Number 93, walked on, and then turned, quite sure that no one followed him. Without hesitation, he moved towards the front door, going up three steep steps to a small porch with a patterned tiled floor. He tried the door, but it was locked. He took out a pen-knife and opened it to a special blade which was in fact a picklock. He thrust this into the key-hole, twisted swiftly, felt the lock click back, and opened the door.

No one inside made any sound.

Rollison stepped right in, and closed the door. What light there was came from the plain glass of the fanlight. As his eyes became adjusted to the gloom he saw that the narrow hall was newly decorated in pale gray water-paint. There was a clean smell, almost an antiseptic one, the kind of astringent odor which came from the frequent and thorough use of modern cleaning aids.

He stood still for at least two minutes, but heard nothing.

There was a fairly large hall, narrowing to a passage which ran alongside the staircase. One door leading off the hall was easy to force. He went through to find a spotless bathroom on one side of a tiny passage, a kitchen with a stainless steel sink, refrigerator and big gas cooker on the other. Beyond this was a comfortably furnished bed-sitting-room.

He returned to the hall, and opened another door to the front room. This was not part of the flat, but obviously a communal lounge, with a dozen armchairs, a 21-inch screen television set in one corner and a large radiogram.

The first floor had a landing and two bed-sitting-rooms, each with a bathroom and separate W.C. Each flatlet" had a tiny kitchenette or pantry, with a stainless steel sink which also served as a hand-basin; a hot-plate, with two rings, a saucepan or two, some cutlery and crockery; any woman living in one of these could fend for herself very comfortably.

To fit the house and redecorate, Rollison calculated must have cost at least four or five hundred pounds a flat; a lot of money had been spent here lately, for there were two flatlet rooms on each of the four floors, and all had the same equipment, fixtures and fittings.

In each were women's clothes; on each dressing-table were make-up accessories and the various oddments one might expect to find when a woman lived on her own.

At the top floor, and the eighth empty flatlet, Rollison hesitated. Here a narrow wooden staircase led to an attic or loft; unless she was up there, Betty Bishop was not in the house. He reminded himself that there had never been more than an outside chance that he would find her here.

"But I'll make quite sure," he said to himself, and started cautiously up the wooden steps, not much more than a ladder. There was a big hatch cover in the ceiling, which moved quite freely when he pushed.

He shifted this aside with great care, until he could climb up into the roof. His head and shoulders were through when he saw the narrow bed behind some sloping rafters and realized that someone lay on it. He climbed over, and stared down at the sleeping figure of a girl.

It was Betty Bishop—the photograph he had seen left no doubt. The deep satisfaction, almost the elation, at having found her faded in anxiety.

Was she sleeping? or drugged? or dead?

He felt very fearful as he crossed to her, and stood looking down. She was tired looking, but pretty. Her eyes and lashes, her forehead and her nose, were like her brother's, but there the likeness ended.

She was breathing. He could see the blanket which covered her, rising and falling, could even see the slight movement of her beautifully shaped lips. It was hard to picture her at one of those machines over which Osgood kept such a tyrannical watch.

She did not stir.

Rollison touched her shoulder, and still she made no movement. He shifted the blanket to one side, saw that she wore a pink short-sleeved nightdress with a puckered neckline, felt for her wrist and drew her arm up so that he could feel her pulse. It was slow and faint, but regular. There was little doubt that she was under sedation, and as far as he could judge she would remain so for an hour or more. He drew the blanket up around her, then moved back to the hole in the floor.

He could telephone for the police, who would arrive in a few minutes; or he could wait until Kate McGuire came home, and try to force her to tell him what she knew.

He was trying to decide what to do, reminding himself that there was no hurry where the girl was concerned, nothing was likely to disturb her, when he heard a sound downstairs—the opening and closing of a door. Every other flatlet had been empty and the back door locked and bolted, so someone had come in at the front.

He listened for footsteps.

They were clear and deliberate, almost certainly a woman's. Rollison crept down the wooden steps, acutely conscious of every creak they made, without closing the hatch. No footsteps sounded on the stairs, but there were movements as if someone was in a ground-floor room. He descended two flights, making hardly a sound, and peered down.

Although he had a foreshortened view, he recognized the woman at once. It was Kate McGuire; the machinist who had approached Osgood so boldly and so menacingly with the long, sharp scissors.

She turned towards the kitchen, and disappeared, her movements brisk and assured. Rollison went down to the ground floor, trying to make up his mind how best to surprise and to unnerve her, and was halfway to the partly open kitchen door when he heard a car pull up outside. There seemed something urgent about this arrival and a faint squeal came from brakes or tires. A door opened, then slammed and footsteps clattered—the footsteps of men in a hurry.

As Rollison backed swiftly into the front lounge, there was a loud knock.

Rollison was as nearly sure as he could be that these men were police. If only they had given him twenty minutes in which to question Kate McGuire——

She must be feeling almost desperately alarmed. But she didn't seem to be alarmed at all as she left the kitchen and walked towards the door, opening it as if she hadn't a care in the world.

KATE McGUIRE

"Good afternoon," said Kate McGuire.

"We are police officers," a man said in a harsh voice, "and we have a warrant to search these premises."

"Then come along in," the woman welcomed. "I won't try to stop you."

Rollison heard the note of laughter in her voice, and warmed to her. The hard-voiced policeman grunted, and three men entered the hall. Rollison was already trying to decide what to say if they searched the room in which he was hiding first, at any moment he expected the door to open wider.

"You'll find what you're looking for up in the attic," Kate declared.

"How do you know what we're looking for?" a man demanded.

"I telephoned you about it," Kate said. "At least, I telephoned Scotland Yard, and that's the same thing, isn't it?"

The man, humorless and dull, grunted again, and soon heavy footsteps sounded on the stairs.

"Do you want me to come?" Kate asked.

"You stay down there."

"It doesn't cost anything to be polite," Kate McGuire protested. "Even for a policeman."

Rollison found himself smiling broadly.

He went to the window, and looked out at the police car parked at the curb. A man was standing by it, so he couldn't simply walk out. It might be possible to escape by the back door, but that would depend on the woman. He waited until the footsteps sounded a long way above, then opened the flat door wider, and stepped into the passage. The street door was ajar, but the policeman out there couldn't see in. The kitchen door was ajar, too, and as Rollison stepped towards it he heard the sound of running water and the rattly noise of a kettle being filled. He pushed the door open wider. Kate McGuire had her back to him as she turned from the sink to the stove. As she placed the kettle on the flames, Rollison said:

"A cup of tea is just what I would like."

She didn't spin round. For a moment she stood absolutely still; then she began to move her hand slowly away from the kettle.

"Surprise, surprise," she said.

"The thing life is full of. You're quite a regular little stool-pigeon, aren't you? First you telephone the Yard about my battle with Ossy, now you tell them about Betty."

"I always like to keep on the right side of the law."

"And on the wrong side of the truth?"

She turned round, slowly. It was the first time he had been able to study her at close range, and his original impressions were now confirmed. In her slightly florid way, she was very striking; handsome rather than beautiful. She had fine, hazel eyes, broad but good features, a Junoesque figure.

"What I say and what I do are *not* your business," she said.

"When you tell the police I attacked Osgood violently, it is my business."

"You were beside yourself," she declared flatly. "At the time you looked as if you didn't know what you were doing."

"I knew what *you* were doing," said Rollison. "And I'll find out what you're up to now."

But even to his own ears, the words sounded empty. He had come hoping to find something which he could use to bring pressure to bear on this woman, and so compel her to talk. For a few minutes up in the loft he had

92

thought the presence here of Betty Bishop was exactly what he needed, but Kate had put an end to such hope as easily as puncturing a toy balloon with a pin. She was smiling at him, as if realizing what was passing through his mind.

"The real question is what you're up to," she said. "Supposing I tell the police I discovered you hiding here?" Her smile broadened, a glow of unmistakable humour shone in her eyes. "They would probably think you had come to see the girl you betrayed."

Rollison said softly: "Yes, wouldn't they?"

"Toff," Kate McGuire said, "I've got you just where I want you. Don't try to pretend I haven't."

"Kate," Rollison said, "just where do you want me?"

"Where you will do what you're told."

"Blackmail, is it?"

"A sort of blackmail, yes."

"Is that why the baby was put on the doorstep?"

"Yes."

"Is that why Osgood came to my flat—to find more reasons for blackmail?"

"Could be."

"How nice to be truthful even if you can't be honest," Rollison said. "And is that why you lied about what happened at the workroom?"

"Yes."

"How did you manage to persuade all the others to lie with you?"

"Everyone will lie if they think it will pay."

"You think so," said Rollison rather ponderously. "All very effective. What do you want?"

"A little moral support."

"You certainly need that," Rollison said drily. "About what?"

"You'll learn in good time."

After a long pause, Rollison remarked: "The kettle's beginning to boil."

93

"I'll make the tea," Kate said. As she turned to do so, footsteps sounded on the stairs, and quite suddenly Rollison realized that he had been oblivious of the police, of everything except what this woman had been saying. "I can tell the police you broke in, or I can say you are my guest," she went on brightly. "Which is it to be?"

Rollison mused aloud: "The first of the blackmail procedure—do what I tell you or I'll charge you with shoplifting."

Teapot in hand, she turned and smiled with quite seductive boldness.

"You've got the point," she agreed.

"Kate McGuire," Rollison said heavily, "a lot of people have thought they could blackmail me and get away with it. They've all been wrong."

"I'm not wrong."

"You are, you know. Tell the police what you like. I don't think they'll take your word against mine."

She didn't stop smiling, but her expression changed slightly, as if she were suddenly doubtful of her power. Before either could speak again, there was a tap at the door. Rollison stepped back, out of sight.

"We've found her," the hard-faced man announced. "We'll send an ambulance for her, and take her away. Meanwhile, I want a statement from you."

"I've already dictated a statement by telephone—the Yard said they would have it typed and send it to me to sign," Kate said. "I let my attic room to a woman I've never seen before, who gave her name as Smith. I thought she was having friends who stayed at night, and when she'd left this lunch-time, I went up to find out what I could. That's when I found the Bishop girl, who'd often been here to see me. Naturally, I telephoned the Yard."

Scepticism was clear in the hard voice of the policeman whom Rollison had heard speaking before, but had not yet seen.

"This woman Smith——"

"She came for one of my larger flatlets, a week ago. She paid a month in advance, and she looked presentable. She said she had just left her husband and had nowhere to stay, and that's exactly the type of tenant I like. I didn't take references. I didn't check her luggage."

"You've got all the answers, I'll say that for you," the policeman growled.

"That's always easy when you tell the truth," Kate said sweetly. "If I leave the front door open for the ambulance men, will you make sure that no one who shouldn't breaks in?"

"No one's going to break in."

"You'd be surprised," Kate said. "I'll be here, if I'm wanted."

She closed the door, turned and smiled broadly at Rollison, and then twisted the key in the lock.

"I suppose you think you've won the first round," she remarked.

"I'd prefer to call it even," said Rollison. "I like the way you handle policemen."

"That's the way I handle all men."

"I'm disappointed. I thought you stuck scissors into the Osgoods of this world."

"Only when I can't get them to do what I want without scissors," she retorted.

"Will Ossy do what you want?"

"If he knows what's good for him," said Kate McGuire. She smiled again. "So will you." She poured out tea, handed Rollison a cup, then lifted a jar with a beautiful high glaze from a shelf and offered it to him; inside were shortbreads. He took one, reflecting on the remarkable naturalness of this woman, and the fact that he found it so easy to be natural with her. Sipping tea, he studied Kate McGuire and wondered what would happen if he could bring Perdita Shortt here at the wave of a hand. How would she and Kate compare?

"Kate," said Rollison, at last.

"Toff," said Kate.

"I will do whatever I must, whether you like it or not."

"We'll see," she said. "I'm serious."

"I can tell you are."

"So will those witnesses be. You can be charged with assault on Osgood"—she did not once use "Ossy" he noticed—"and there will be ten times the number of witnesses needed to convict you."

"It's a case for the Assizes," Rollison pointed out.

She hadn't expected that remark.

"What do you mean?"

"I mean that there would be a quick hearing, I would get a remand on bail, then another hearing and another remand; finally, the case would be sent to the Old Bailey for a trial by jury instead of summarily by a magistrate. I doubt if it would be included in the Calendar until July, say—possibly the long vacation would postpone it until October. Long before then I would know how you persuaded your seamstresses to lie, so the police would simply withdraw the case."

"You're far too optimistic," she said, but obviously she had been shaken again.

"The other thing can't be laughed off so easily."

"What other thing?"

Her eyes suddenly danced, and she raised her voice and sang: "Hi, Pop!"

Rollison chuckled.

"Did you put that note in my car?"

"One of the girls did it for me."

"Kate."

"Yes, Toff?"

"You are a very scheming woman."

"I take that as a compliment."

"It's meant as a compliment as well as an accusation," Rollison said. He paused when more footsteps sounded outside, then realized that the ambulance men had arrived. He kept his voice low as he went on: "You know as well as I do that you can't do me any harm by spreading it about that I'm Betty Bishop's lover. No one who knows me would believe for a moment that if I fathered a child I'd leave the girl in the lurch. Betty herself could swear it was I, and no one who matters to me would believe her. If I were married I might be blackmailed, if she were married I might either be blackmailed or scared into a pay-off. But I'm not and she's not. The most you could hope for is that I might be shamed, but shame would only come out of a guilty conscience. You're too intelligent to be unaware of all this, so you haven't yet told me what you're up to."

After a long pause, during which her smile faded and she became very straight-faced and almost grim, Kate said:

"I'll tell you, when I'm ready."

"Kate," Rollison said, "do you remember what happened to Mario Bishop?"

She caught her breath, then said bitterly: "Yes, I remember."

Rollison said very softly: "He lay in a drunken stupor on his lonely bed, and someone crept up the stairs and into the room, and killed."

Kate gasped: "Don't!"

"Sensitive, are you?" Rollison said. "Then perhaps there's hope for you yet. If it weren't for that cold blooded murder I might play the game your way, but murder was done, and I want to find the killer, as well as find the man or woman who lied about me and Bishop's daughter. Who killed Mario Bishop, Kate?"

"Don't ask *me!*" She took a deep breath, as if to regain her poise, but the sudden switch to Bishop's murder had shaken her badly. "I don't know anything about it."

"Does Osgood?"

"He was at the factory——" she began hastily.

"Oh no, he wasn't," Rollison said. "Nor were you. No factory starts before eight o'clock, and I'm pretty sure Mario was killed two or three hours before that. You could have killed him, so could Osgood, so could Parks."

"So could Mario's son!"

"Oh yes," Rollison said. "He could have killed his father, and if he did we will prove it, but he's not my favorite suspect. Kate——"

"I tell you I don't know who cut his throat." But now she was really frightened.

"And I don't believe you," Rollison said. "Any more than I believe you've told me what you really want with me. Kate——"

"Stop saying Kate like that!"

"Kate," repeated Rollison in a cold, clipped voice, "Mario was murdered between five and six o'clock this morning. The body was discovered, by me, at eight o'clock. The news is in the newspapers, but not the fact that his throat was cut, so you can't have read about that. How did you know how he was killed . . . *Kate?*"

12

HELD FOR QUESTIONING

Kate McGuire stood very still in front of Rollison, a kind of defiance in her manner. It was possible that she was putting on an act, pretending to a mood she did not really feel, simply to mislead him, but he did not believe this was true. He had the impression that the way he had talked of the murder had not only taken her by surprise but found a weak link in her armour of self-confidence.

"Well, how did you hear about the manner of Bishop's murder?" Rollison insisted.

"A little bird told me," Kate said tartly.

"Grow up, Kate!"

As he spoke he realized he had said the same thing to Perdita. Kate's reaction was much the same; her eyes sparked, and she clenched her hands by her sides as if trying to control her anger.

"It's time you left," she said. "You've outstayed your welcome."

Rollison stood watching her for what must have seemed a long time. There were slow movements in the passage, the closing of the front door, followed by the sound of the ambulance moving off.

"Now that it's all clear I can go," Rollison said. He nodded, smiled and turned towards the door. He half expected Kate to stop him, or call him back, but she neither moved nor looked round. He set the lock on the front door so that it did not latch, and closed the door firmly.

Outside on the street, he glanced up and down. No policemen were in sight, no one took any notice of him. He saw no one at the front window as he turned away, but after walking twenty yards or so, he stopped and swung on his heel, in the manner of a man who had suddenly realized he had forgotten something, and strode back to Number 93, keeping close to the houses. He took the steps in two long strides, and pushed the door open gently.

". . . you mean he's still there?" Kate was saying into the telephone. "What . . . I tell you Rollison suspects me . . . No, he doesn't know about you, but he knows I know something about it . . . Yes . . . Yes . . . *No!*" That was an explosive cry from the heart. "No, I don't . . . It's all going haywire . . . Well, we can only wait until we see what's happened . . . Yes, send him here if they do let him go, but they can't believe . . . All right. I'll be in all the evening."

There was a *ting* as she replaced the receiver.

Rollison fought back the impulse to ask what it was "they" couldn't believe. She had at least one confidant, and it might be Osgood; certainly she was expecting someone who might come here. He wished that he had arranged for one of Ebbutt's men, or even for Jolly, to be at hand and watch this house, but he hadn't.

There was a telephone kiosk at the end of the street.

He crept out of the house again and walked briskly to the kiosk; a young girl was speaking, obviously near tears, and oblivious of him or of anyone else who stood near by. She might be a long time there. He did not want to make his presence too noticeable, nor did he want to miss the chance of having next use of the box.

He saw a small Austin approaching, pearl gray, like his second car which Jolly often used; now if only it were Jolly——

It *was* Jolly!

The car pulled in and Rollison bent down quickly as Jolly opened the window.

"Trouble?" demanded Rollison quite sure that it was.

"Of a kind, sir."

"What kind?"

"The man Osgood is very gravely ill," Jolly reported. "He is in hospital undergoing a major brain operation—apparently he suffered a cerebral hemorrhage caused by a severe blow on the head which did very little superficial damage, and wasn't noticed. Mr. Grice telephoned to say he wishes to talk to you about this forthwith. I told him I had no idea where you were, and he simply requested me to advise you of this situation as soon as possible."

Rollison opened the passenger door, and got in.

"Were you followed?"

"No, sir."

"Then Grice was giving you a chance to warn me before I was picked up for questioning. Jolly——"

"Sir?"

"I think this is serious."

"I could not agree with you more, sir."

"If Osgood should die——" Rollison began, then hesitated.

"You are likely to face a charge of manslaughter at the very least." Jolly looked grave, and his gloved hands on the wheel were very tense. "And if you were under such a charge, even on bail, there would be restrictions on your movements."

"Yes," Rollison agreed. "The question is——" When he broke off again, Jolly made no attempt to prompt him. "The question is whether Osgood was injured before I went to the factory, or after."

"Didn't you say that he seemed in normal health?"

"Yes," agreed Rollison. "But the early effect of a serious head injury might be similar to that of concussion—a victim can behave normally, although he doesn't afterwards remember what he's been doing. Still—I think he was normal enough, except——"

Again Jolly waited patiently for Rollison to continue.

"Except that he scared easily," said Rollison at last. "Too easily."

"Perhaps he had a lot to be frightened of," suggested Jolly.

"Yes. Jolly——"

"Sir?"

"I don't want to believe what I think I should believe."

"What is that, sir?"

"Unless Osgood was injured before I went to Ticky's, he was injured while with me. There's only one place where that could have happened."

"Ebbutt's Gymnasium?" said Jolly.

"Yes. He was out of my sight there for at least twenty minutes. I don't like this at all."

"Nor do I, sir."

"If one of Ebbutt's men injured Osgood, then there is at least one we can't trust, and until we know which one, we can't use any of them."

"I agree with you absolutely," Jolly said. "In fact, I have not alerted any of Ebbutt's men to our tasks in case you shared my own anxiety."

"I'm glad you didn't. So we're on our own."

"We are indeed," said Jolly, speaking almost as if he relished the fact. "And we have to establish a list of priorities soon, sir."

"What do you put first?" inquired Rollison.

"Finding the common denominator among all the things that have happened," said Jolly without hesitation. "Some of them seem quite unconnected, but there must surely be a connection—between what happened at Ticky's and the Bishop family, for instance."

"I can tell you of one connection," Rollison said. "No less than Kate McGuire." He told Jolly what had happened, and saw Jolly's tension relax, as if this were good news. "So we have just one straight line—the baby—the Bishops—Osgood—Ticky's—Kate McGuire. *Very* interesting, but not yet very helpful. I wonder who she was talking to. I hoped it was Osgood, but——"

"Osgood won't talk again for days, if he ever talks at

all," Jolly said somberly. "The one person who might be of some help is Sydney Bishop, and he is still being questioned at Scotland Yard. I asked Mr. Grice whether he would be detained, and received a noncommittal answer."

"Kate was talking about Syd and was worried about him," Rollison mused. "The Bishops—Betty—the baby—Osgood—Kate—Ticky's. The only missing cypher is the man Parks—Punchy Parks—who came to the flat with Osgood. The most worrying factor is doubt about at least one of Ebbutt's men."

"I don't see it quite like that, sir. The most worrying factor is that you may be charged with manslaughter or murder."

"You really believe that, don't you," Rollison said heavily. "Grice must have pitched the note high."

"He most certainly impressed on me the gravity of the situation. My impression was that he felt that if there was anything you wanted to do urgently, you should do it." Jolly turned to face Rollison, and there was no shadow of doubt that he was worried. "I'm particularly troubled about the Ebbutt development, sir, because I thought it might be advisable for you to spend a day or two with him."

"On the run," said Rollison, heavily.

"Until we know more about the situation, it might be advisable for you not to be readily available."

Rollison said very slowly and deliberately: "No, Jolly. No. Not in this affair. If I disappear the police would have to put out a general call, the Press would have a super-Roman holiday, and I would never live the laughter down. Not with that *Hi Pop* signature tune. I can afford a dozen defeats, but must not be made a fool of in public even once. But cheer up, sobersides! There's a funny side to this if we can only see it. Perhaps it's the way I'm going to put my head into the lion's mouth."

With a deep sigh of resignation, Jolly said: "So you are going to Scotland Yard, sir?"

"And you're going to drive me there," Rollison told him. Then he clapped a hand on Jolly's arm. "Give me five minutes first, I want to telephone the *Globe*."

"Micky?"

"Hallo," said Wiseman of the *Globe*. "I hear you're in even worse trouble than you were last time we talked."

"I'm not in trouble, I'm going to get a young man out of it," Rollison said.

"Which young man?"

"Syd Bishop."

"You mean you're going to the Yard?" Wiseman sounded startled.

"Yes. He's been there quite long enough," said Rollison brightly. "The police must either charge him, or let him go."

Wiseman's voice was deep with satisfaction.

"Now *that's* a story. The old crusading Toff again, Defender of the Poor and Helpless, carrying the war into the Enemy's Camp. Is that the angle you're asking me to use?"

"Yes."

"Like me to give it to the television news-rooms, too."

"Very much."

"Keep me posted," Wiseman said jubilantly. "Anything else?"

"People keep singing *Hi, Pop!* to me."

Wiseman chuckled.

"They do?"

"Now if the *Globe* put up a prize for a pop song of that title, we'd get the public in the right mood," Rollison prophesied hopefully. "I volunteer to serve on the panel of judges."

"If I can swing my masters, I'll do exactly that," Wiseman promised. "I can tell you one thing. The police found Betty Bishop, and she's in St. Mary's Hospital doing well." He gave an explosive laugh. " 'Bye, Pop!" he chortled, and rang off.

The Toff had for years been a frequent visitor to the headquarters of the Metropolitan Police force, with whom, over much of this period, he had been *persona grata*. This evening, he felt that most of the officials who saw him seemed somewhat surprised, and others whom he passed on the way to Grice's office appeared positively astonished. He tapped on the door and opened it on the same instant. Grice looked up from his desk.

"Good God!" he exclaimed.

"Hi, Bill," said Rollison, beaming. "I hear you've been inquiring after my health."

"Why didn't you tell me you were coming?"

"Your grapevine isn't working, obviously," said Rollison. "Where's young Bishop?"

"That's not your business."

"Come off it, Bill."

"You've plenty to worry about without worrying about him."

"Bill," said Rollison softly, "I think I need Syd Bishop to find out the truth of certain allegations leveled against me, so I want to talk to him."

"You can't."

"Have you charged him?"

"That's not your business, either."

Rollison, still standing, looked down upon the Yard man, wondering uneasily what was passing through his mind, and slowly raised a forefinger.

"May I use your telephone?"

"Why?"

"To call Syd Bishop's solicitors."

"He hasn't any solicitors."

"He has from this moment. Scott, English and Scott, who also represent me."

"I tell you that you've plenty to worry about without getting any further involvement with young Bishop," Grice said sharply. "Parricide isn't a nice crime."

"False charges aren't nice, either."

"Rolly," Grice said, using the diminutive with an obvious effort. "I can't make my warning any clearer. I ought to have you in for questioning about Osgood as it is—if he should die, I'll have to."

"There's something else you can do," Rollison said.

"What's that?"

"Find who attacked him."

"You thick-witted fool, a *hundred* witnesses saw you attack him! This isn't something you can laugh off!"

"Oh, I don't know," Rollison said. "A laugh is worth a thousand tears in any state of the market. May I make that call?"

"If you want to force me to charge *you* now—go ahead."

"All I want is to force you to release Syd Bishop, or else charge him," Rollison said. "And if you won't do either, let me have a talk with him on his own."

He did not really believe he would get anywhere. This was like everything had proved to be in this affair, a dead end. It was almost as if some kind of fate dictated that he should be frustrated at every turn.

He shrugged that thought aside as absurd.

Grice was studying him intently. He knew the Superintendent as well as he knew anyone, and would never have the slightest doubt of Grice's goodwill. But why was Grice so grim and dour about this? Was it simply because he believed the evidence of the seamstresses and machinists at Ticky's? It wasn't the first time that Grice had been sour, of course, but in the past it had always been because he thought Rollison was taking advantage of their long friendship.

Suddenly Grice said: "I'll let you talk to young Bishop, but I'll want to be in the next room, where I can hear all that's being said. Bishop needn't know you're being overheard. Will you settle for that?"

Instantly Rollison agreed. "Yes. Thanks, Bill."

Inwardly he thought: "Grice doesn't want me to get legal aid yet, so he can't be very sure of his case against young Syd."

13

FEAR

"Do you know who killed your father?" Rollison demanded.

"I've told you time and time again, *no!*"

"I still don't believe you."

"You're as bad as the bloody cops!" Young Bishop's voice was unsteady and very hoarse. He looked infinitely more tired than he had that morning, and he hadn't shaved, hadn't combed that luxuriant black hair. His skin-tight jeans were spotless and his black-leather jacket was like a straight-jacket. It was loosened at the neck, and unzipped far enough down to show the top of a white singlet or T-shirt. "That's the truth about you, you're as bad as the cops!"

"Was it Osgood?" demanded Rollison.

"*I don't know!*"

"Syd, you know a lot more than you're admitting," Rollison said, and feeling sure that he was right. But what was the boy lying about? Did he know the murderer, or did he simply suspect someone?

"Listen, Toff," Bishop said stiffly, "I didn't kill my old man, I don't know anything about it. All I want to do is to get out of here and find my sister. My sister—remember her? *My sister!* She might be dead——"

Rollison barked: "Why do you say that?"

"It's obvious! For crying out loud, it's obvious!"

"No, it isn't. What makes you think she might be dead?"

"*She could die in child-birth, couldn't she?*"

"Oh," said Rollison, blankly. "That's what you mean." Why did he so often relate death with murder? "You needn't worry about her, Syd," he soothed.

"That's easy for you to say, you don't know her. That's if you're telling the truth."

"She's all right, Syd."

"*How do you know?*"

"I've seen her. The police found her. She's quite all right."

He had never seen a greater effect on any man. One moment Syd was stifling his rage, wild with anxiety, even fear; the next, he was staring at Rollison, his eyes huge and rounded, his whole expression changed to one of pleading. He put his hand forward and touched Rollison's arm.

"You—*saw* her?"

"Yes."

"You wouldn't lie to me."

"She's all right, Syd, I promise you. The police took her to hospital—the St. Mary's, the same hospital as her baby."

"Oh, thank God," Syd Bishop said in a broken voice, "*thank God.*" Tears welled up in his eyes. Suddenly, savagely, he dashed his hand across his face, and his voice became loud and harsh. "So she's okay, so that's what you say. I want to see for myself. Can you get me out of here?"

"I can try. You can get yourself out of here if you tell me or the police who killed your father."

"*I don't know!*" insisted Syd doggedly. "I was out with Ossy, so it couldn't have been him and it couldn't have been me. *I* don't know anything, I swear it. I swear it, I tell you!"

"Bill," Rollison said to Grice, "I should let him go."

"And what would you like me to do after that?" Grice asked sarcastically.

"Let me follow him."

"You've got yourself into enough trouble about this

109

affair already," Grice objected. "Do you think he knows anything at all?"

"I think he suspects someone—or at least guesses."

"You may be right. If we let him go, and you lose him —what then?"

"You can pick him up again, can't you?"

Grice stared moodily at Rollison, obviously with something on his mind which he had not yet disclosed. They were alone in his office, where Rollison's back was towards the Embankment, the plane trees not yet in bud and the smooth-running river.

Abruptly Grice said: "All right. But I've warned you. If Osgood dies we'll have to pick you up. As it is, I want a statement from you about what happened at Ticky's."

"I'll dictate that in five minutes," Rollison said. "Or write it in ten. "

"Write it," Grice said, and pushed a foolscap-sized pad across the desk. Rollison wrote swiftly, stating the simple facts, then handed the pad back.

Grice read it carefully, going over some sentences several times. Then he looked up, and said:

"The women who were interviewed—seven altogether —state quite clearly that you made a violent attack on Osgood, and that you were stopped only by their protests."

After a long pause, Rollison said softly: "There's something badly wrong, Bill. It's not true."

"Seven to one makes pretty convincing evidence."

"Yes," Rollison agreed. "Bill—this shop-lifting you suspect Osgood of organizing. Have you anything on him at all?"

"All but absolute, irrefutable proof for a jury."

"Oh. Do you know how many people are involved?"

"Probably dozens, Grice said. "But all we have to work on is from three witnesses. If you know anything at all, you must tell us at once."

"If I ever find out anything, I'll tell you," Rollison promised.

"And get it into your head—I've warned you how dangerous your position is."

"Yes," Rollison said softly. "You've warned me. Now make sure Syd leaves by the Embankment gates, will you?"

"All right," Grice said.

A few minutes later, Rollison was sitting at the wheel of the little gray Austin, a car as unlike his Bentley as a car could be. Five minutes later still, young Bishop strode out of the Yard on to the Embankment, and looked up and down, as if for a taxi. One came along, and he hailed it.

Rollison followed.

The taxi swung round at the end of Northumberland Avenue, and turned towards Westminster Bridge, then Parliament Square and the Houses of Parliament. Beyond that Gothic pile, the huge modern block at Millbank seemed like a glance at tomorrow. Traffic was thick in the early rush hour. The taxi turned left, over Lambeth Bridge, and Rollison followed, very thoughtful now.

Lambeth—Kennington—Camberwell.

There seemed little doubt where the youth was heading, and in two minutes all doubt was stifled, because the taxi turned into Circle Road and pulled up outside Number 93. Syd Bishop sprang from it; obviously he had paid the taxi-driver, who moved off at once. Rollison slowed down twenty yards from Kate McGuire's house, squeezed the Austin into a parking space and crossed the road to Number 93.

The door was locked.

Rollison did exactly what he had done that afternoon, opened it with a picklock and stepped inside. As soon as the door opened he heard Syd Bishop yelling:

"You bitch, it's all your fault. You killed him, you——"

"Don't be a fool! Keep away from me!" Kate cried. There was alarm in her voice.

"*You killed him.* You drove him crazy, and then you killed him!"

"Get away!" screamed Kate, but the words ended in a choking gurgle.

Rollison flung open the kitchen door as Kate was forced backwards over the steel sink. Bishop's hands were about her neck, his body pressing close to hers, and Rollison could see the power in the way he strained against her, the way his muscles bulged even inside the shiny sleeves of his jacket. Kate was clutching ineffectively at his wrists.

Rollison took a step forward and chopped the side of his right hand down on the nape of Syd Bishop's neck. The single sharp blow was enough. Syd's strength seemed to ebb from him, his hold on Kate slackened and his body sagged. Rollison took him by the shoulders and thrust him to one side; he fell against the gas stove, and reeled there, helpless. Kate McGuire leaned so far forward now that she seemed likely to topple head first. She was gasping for breath, her hands at her throat as if to ease the pain. Rollison put his arms round her and made her move out of the kitchen and into the front room, which was empty. He helped her to lie at full length on a couch, unzipped her dress at the side, found the zipper of her girdle, and loosened that, too; her flesh was very warm. He stood back and looked down at her, then turned and went to the kitchen. Syd was beginning to straighten up, the paroxysms of rage past. Rollison said roughly:

"If you try to move out of this flat, I'll wring your neck!"

He opened cupboards and found whisky and brandy, motioned to the whisky for Syd, and took some brandy into the front room. He put the glass to Kate's lips, and she began to sip. In a few minutes her color was better and she was sitting up.

"I'll be back," Rollison said, and went out.

Syd Bishop had opened the refrigerator and poured himself some milk, the whisky bottle stood untouched. There was nervous defiance in his manner as he looked at Rollison, and perhaps a touch of shame.

"What got into you?" demanded Rollison. He expected an explosive: "None of your business!" or something similar, but instead Syd moistened his lips and said:

"I ought to have strangled the bitch."

"Why?"

"I hate her guts."

"Did you hate your father's guts?"

Syd Bishop cried, as if in anguish: "No, but *she* did! She drove him to drink, if it hadn't been for her he would have been alive—*she* drove him to drink, I tell you."

"I can imagine she could do that to a man," Rollison encouraged.

"He never knew where he was with her. Even before my mother died he was having an affair with her—blow hot, blow cold. One minute she couldn't do enough for him, the next she was going around with other men and laughing in his face. I tell you it's true."

"I can believe it," Rollison said. "But would she kill him?"

"She knows who did. I'm sure she knows—Rollison, listen! I don't know what it was, but he'd got something on her, and on Osgood. He used to have to do anything they told him. She led him a hell of a life, but he had to dance to any tune *she* played. Why sometimes he used to have to beg her to let him have a bottle of *that* bloody poison!" Syd glared at the whisky. "Then suddenly he started to get all the money he wanted—and he began telling her *and* Osgood where to get off. He'd got them where he wanted them, that's why he was killed. I'm sure of it."

"Why didn't you tell the police about this?" Rollison wanted to know.

"That's *my* business."

"You mean it's a family feud?"

"I mean I can settle my own affairs. I don't have to squeal to the cops if I want something done."

"Listen, Syd," Rollison said reasoningly, "you're saying that your father was blackmailing Kate McGuire and Osgood, so that they gave him all the whisky he wanted, and got off his back."

"So what? That's the truth!"

"Then why did you believe Osgood when he told you I knew your sister?"

"The fact that he was a swine didn't make him a liar!"

"Don't try to fool me any more," Rollison warned. "When you came to my flat you believed him. Something happened between the time you tried to break my neck and the time you tried to break Kate's. What was it?"

Syd made a sobbing sound as he gasped:

"They killed my father! They must have done!"

Whether there was reason in what he said or not hardly mattered; certainly if he believed Kate McGuire and Osgood had anything to do with his father's murder it could explain his attitude now. The very nature of the youth, his background and his environment, made credible his refusal to talk freely with the police.

One thing seemed certain: Kate *could* have killed Mario Bishop. Rollison recalled the way she had advanced on Osgood with the scissors——

Here was fundamental contradiction, though; that Kate and Osgood appeared to work together, and yet they had been on different sides at Ticky's.

Had they? Or had Kate been putting on an act? Was

114

the *volte-face* by the women and girls there due to her influence?

"Syd," Rollison said abruptly, "I'm not the baby's father. Have you any idea who is?"

"Not the foggiest," Syd answered, sounding as if he were in anguish. "If I knew who it was, I would——"

"Break his neck, I know," said Rollison drily. "Keep thinking like that and one day you'll kill someone and spend the rest of your life in prison. Go to my flat and wait there for me. My man will let you in, and probably you'll see Mrs. Shortt. Behave yourself."

He thought Syd would protest, but was wrong.

He wondered if the youth would really go to Gresham Terrace, and decided that he probably would, so as soon as the front door had closed, he picked up the white telephone in the kitchen, called Jolly and spoke briefly and to the point.

"I will see to the young man, sir," Jolly promised. "I gather that the outcome of your meeting with Mr. Grice was reasonably satisfactory."

"Not bad at all," Rollison confirmed. "Is Mrs. Shortt there?"

"She left about half an hour ago, without saying where she was going."

"Did she say she would be back?"

"Oh yes," said Jolly. "And she brought an overnight case this afternoon, so I think she is planning to stay for a few days. Is it in order for me to cater on that assumption?"

"Get nothing but the best," ordered Rollison.

"I invariably get the best, sir," said Jolly, with mild reproof.

Smiling, Rollison went back to the front room, surprised that Kate had stayed there so long, and half prepared to find that she had left. But she had not. In fact she was zipping up her dress.

"Fully recovered?" asked Rollison, cheerfully.

"I'm all right," said Kate, in a subdued voice. "Where's that murderous little whelp?"

"Gone to cool his heels."

"I'd cool him over if I had my way."

"He'd break your neck with pleasure because he thinks you seduced his father, and then connived at his murder," Rollison said. "Don't expect him to have kindly thoughts about you."

Unexpectedly Kate's gaze softened, and she moved closer to Rollison, one hand outstretched.

"Poor little devil," she said. "He had a drunken father who made life hell for his invalid mother. He blamed everyone but Mario, but at heart he knew that everything was Mario's fault. Mario was so—beguiling. He fooled me, and I tried to help him, tried to make him fight, to win back some self-respect, but it didn't work. He was so sodden with whisky he was like a sponge, whisky was the only thing that could ever seduce him."

"Yet he was able to blackmail you," Rollison said.

"Blackmail, my eye. I stopped trying with him, that's all. If he wanted to drink himself to death, why should I stop him?"

"Why keep him supplied with whisky?"

"I don't know where he got his whisky or his money from," Kate declared. "The kid may think I do, but I don't."

For the first time since Rollison had started to talk, Kate looked away from him. Following her gaze to the window, he saw a woman getting out of a taxi opposite the front door. First came long, slender legs, then her body.

She leaned inside the cab for a suitcase, then drew away and straightened up.

Rollison gaped at Perdita, who looked first at the front door of Number 93, then at the window from which Rollison had seen her.

14

NEW TENANT

Rollison moved swiftly to one side, glancing at Kate McGuire to judge whether she had noticed his reaction; she did not appear to have done so. Perdita paid off the taxi and stepped to the front door.

"Old friend?" asked Rollison.

"I've never seen her before," Kate said. "I expect she wants a flatlet."

All Rollison could say was: "Oh."

The front door bell rang.

"Mr. Rollison," Kate said with an unexpected burst of feeling, "if you hadn't come in when you did, I think Syd would have killed me. I won't forget that ever."

She went out.

A moment later, Rollison heard the front door open and the two women talking.

"Good evening."

"Good evening."

"Are you the proprietress?"

"Yes."

"I'm told you might have a vacant flat."

"Yes, I have. Would you like to see it?"

"Please——"

The front door closed, footsteps sounded on the stairs, then immediately above Rollison's head. These lasted for some time; then one set of footsteps sounded on the stairs, and Kate returned.

"I've seen her before somewhere," she said. "She seems rather nice."

"She's very nice," said Rollison. "So is her photograph in the *Daily Pic*."

Kate frowned, as if baffled, and then exclaimed: "*Your* woman!"

Rollison chuckled.

"I don't think she would put it quite like that. Kate—you really mean you won't forget that I saved your neck."

"I really mean it," Kate said fervently.

"Don't tell Perdita that I've been here, then, but tell me what she gets up to."

After a moment, Kate McGuire said rather huskily: "Toff, you haven't forgotten that our interests conflict, have you? We're at war."

After a momentary pause, Rollison put up his hands in mock surrender.

"I had forgotten. Thanks for reminding me. But don't let any harm come to Perdita, will you?"

"She said her name was Shaw—Phyllis Shaw."

"Then don't let any harm come to Phyllis Shaw," said Rollison. "Why do you work at Ticky's if you own a place like this?"

"Because I get good money from Ticky's. I need to. I've bought this house and turned it into flats, but there's still something owing," Kate answered. "One day I shall want to retire, and live on what this place brings in. And then there's the social aspect—this kind of flatlet is ideal for single women, so I'm helping poor lonely souls to keep away from big bad Toffs."

"I see," Rollison said, admiringly. "What a woman! All right, Kate McGuire." He turned to the door, and asked over his shoulder: "Where can I find Punchy Parks?"

"I talked to him only an hour or so ago," Kate said. "He was at Mallow's Club, that's where he spends a lot of his time."

As he left the house in the gathering dusk, Rollison wondered whether she was very, very subtle; whether in fact she knew he had overheard her telephone conversation and so had deliberately named Parks, or whether she was carrying on the battle in her own devious way; whether, even when she had appeared to be troubled and put out of countenance, she had been fooling him.

He went across to the Austin, and glanced up at Perdita's window. He did not see her, but there was no certainty that she hadn't noticed him. He drove off, very thoughtful indeed.

Perdita had spoken, on arrival, as if she were a stranger to Kate, but the whole affair could have been cleverly stage-managed just to fool him; the two women might possibly be conspiring together, incredible though it seemed.

Perdita—widow of a South African gold-mining millionaire, who hadn't lived in England since her childhood? It *was* nonsense.

Yet the doubt remained——

It was quite dark when he pulled up outside Mallow's Club, and beginning to rain. He found a parking-place a few yards from the doorway of the old warehouse building which stood solitary and bleak against two empty sites on either side. Opposite was a bowling alley, garish with bright lights. Here a dim glow shone over the door, on which was blazoned the name *Mallow's*, in large black letters against a ground of whitened glass. A single gas lamp hung from a bracket on the wall over the door. Two men lounged; representatives of the loiterers who habitually hang around boxing clubs. Rollison hunched his shoulders against the rain, and went inside. Neither of the men moved towards, or spoke to, him. Inside there was a dingy-looking passage, also lit by gas, green paint peeling off brick walls. The thudding of gloves on punch-balls or torsos, came clearly, and even in the passage there was the smell of embrocation oil and sweating bodies.

A man appeared in the doorway.

Rollison did not know how it had happened, but he felt sure that the loiterers had sent some kind of warning.

The man's manner was aggressive and hostile as he blocked the doorway; given another six inches in height he would have been massive indeed; as it was, his forbidding manner would have frightened many.

"What do you want?" he demanded.

"Punchy Parks," Rollison answered politely.

"He's not here."

"Are you sure?"

"I said he's not here, and that's that. Get to hell out of it."

There was more to his attitude than appeared on the surface. This block of a man was there to make sure he couldn't get in—perhaps to prevent him from seeing Parks, perhaps someone else.

"Oh," said Rollison, as if nonplussed and disappointed. He half turned, then spun round like lightning, catching the man off guard. He thrust him back into the room, sprang inside and looked round.

Over by the door marked GENTS was rubbery-faced Rube from Ebbutt's gymnasium; next to him was Punchy Parks.

As Rollison recognized both men, the one behind him made a growling noise in his throat, and launched himself in attack. Rollison first sensed, then saw him coming, and made a back for him; he went flying over Rollison's head, but this was barely a taste of victory. On that instant, he saw men ganging up, obviously to attack him; and there were others from the passage behind him, as well as those in front. Through the crowd he glimpsed Punchy Parks move away from Rube towards an Indian or Pakistani.

Someone said: "Kill him."

It could have been said extravagantly and be an idle threat—but Rollison did not believe this was the case. Without dreaming of it he had walked into acute and deadly danger. He was completely surrounded now, and if they attacked he wouldn't have a chance.

Another man called out: "Give him what he gave Ossy!"

They were drawing nearer, a dozen menacing men, some stripped to the waist, some fully dressed. Two wore boxing gloves; on another man's fist was a glint of metal and the spikes of a knuckle-duster.

Rollison stood absolutely still.

He did not see how he could save himself, unless by this pose he could discourage them from attacking him at all—but he knew there was no real likelihood of that among so many; it might have worked with three or four.

A man said viciously: "What are we waiting for?"

An Indian club hurtled through the air, missing Rollison's head by inches and another came straight at his face. He grabbed it by the thin end, and flung it back, so startling the nearer men that they dodged to one side. On that instant he saw one hope: the parallel bars. These were ranged along one wall with the passage door in between. As another club flew, he snatched at it, and it struck his wrist painfully; he winced, but caught the next and used it like a flail.

Men swayed back out of reach, but there was no hope of reaching the doorway, which was jammed tight. He leapt forward, and two men fell, leaving a space through which he could reach the bars. He swung himself up these with such agility that no one could stop him before he reached a horizontal ladder, then twisted round to face the seething mob below.

He had gained a few minutes, but little more, for they could hurl clubs at him, hurl any kind of missile, and he could not dodge. Too late, he realized that he might have been better off on one of the climbing ropes; he could have swung over their heads on that. But the ropes had been out of reach in any case. For a few seconds there was a hush which fell upon everyone, while Rollison looked down on the sea of faces, the lean, the fat, the old, the young, the ugly, the scowling, the smiling, the handsome. He recognized several of them, with a sense of shock—men who had been at Ticky's factory.

How significant was that?

What did it matter? He could never turn any such significance to advantage.

"*Kill him!*" a man screeched, and a second one leapt up, clutching at his ankle. He felt a sharp pain, and then a crushing blow as a knuckle-duster punched on his instep. A club struck the bar close to his right hand, stinging his fingers. It could only be a matter of minutes, now.

He heard a whistle, high-pitched and loud, from somewhere outside, and two or three of the men glanced towards the open door. The whistle shrilled again, as if in warning, and a man shouted:

"The cops!"

"Cops!"

"My God, the police——"

Then there came a great thudding and clattering outside in the street, men were shouting, others were swearing. Some of those in the room swung round towards the door, others, having gained it, were already rushing out into the street.

The *police?* Or——

Suddenly Rollison saw Punchy Parks, not far away from him. In Punchy's hand was a knife. Beside him was another swarthy-skinned man, the Indian or Pakistani, who also held a knife—by the blade. Before Rollison had realized the extent of his danger the knife was flung at him, a glinting silvery streak. He darted his head to one side, heard the sickening sound of the blade burying itself in the wood of a bar, only an inch from him. A second knife came, and he saw yet another in the swarthy man's hand.

There was only one thing for Rollison to do; he jumped.

The last thing he saw before jumping was huge Bill

Ebbutt, in the doorway, tossing a man aside as if he were a bag of feathers. On Ebbutt's heels were others from the Blue Dog gymnasium——

Rollison hit the floor, knocking the swarthy-skinned man down. He fell on his right shoulder, expecting a thrust from a knife or the crunching force of a toe-cap on his skull. He was vividly reminded of the way Osgood must have been struck over the head as a heavy blow descended on his temple, and felt a spasm of fear as he lost consciousness.

There was light, there was a confusion of sounds, a whistling close by. Rollison's eyes were half closed. His head throbbed in agony, and there was vivid pain in his chest and ribs.

A man wheezed: "You'll be okay, Mr. Ar. Don't worry; you'll be okay."

Bill Ebbutt; bless Bill Ebbutt!

"Don't try to move, we want to make sure you haven't got any busted ribs," said Ebbutt. "Gabby'll be here in a moment."

Rollison opened his eyes.

Ebbutt was squatting on a three-legged stool, looking like an enormous balloon. About him several fights were going on, and at least four men were stretched out on the floor, unconscious. Two others stood near the wall, blood streaming from wounds in their faces. Some of the parallel bars were broken; Indian clubs, boxing gloves, stools and chairs littered the wooden floor as if a hurricane had roared through.

Rollison was on his back, with a rug beneath him.

The little trainer from Ebbutt's gymnasium came across, and bent over Rollison.

"We've been watching Mallow's ever since we knew Osgood was mixed up in this," Ebbutt was saying. "Didn't like some of the things old Rube Rubber Mouth was doing, he'd palled up with Osgood, and been too flush with his dough lately, so we kept an eye on him,

123

too. When we knew he'd come over here tonight we were at action stations, Mr. Ar. Then I had a phone call from one of my boys saying he'd seen you, so we didn't lose any time."

"Bill," Rollison said, "I doubt if I'll ever be able to thank you."

"You've thanked us in advance a hundred times," Ebbutt declared.

Gabby, meanwhile, was feeling Rollison's ribs—a careful and yet thorough probing. The skin was tender, but Rollison felt none of the sharp pain which would indicate a fracture. Gabby took a dark-blue bottle of embrocation from his hip pocket, and began to massage, firmly and yet gently.

"Any special spot, Mr. Ar?"

"No. It's just hell all over."

"Shouldn't take on fifty at a time!" Gabby was disapproving.

"Why didn't you come to us first?" Ebbutt asked, and then he answered himself: "You knew Osgood must have been clobbered at my place, I s'pose, and didn't know who you could trust. Fair enough, Mr. Ar, but you can trust us all now."

Gabby's pressure seemed to be getting firmer and firmer; and more painful.

"Have you seen Punchy Parks?" Rollison asked.

"He got away on a motor-scooter," Ebbutt said. "So did the other basket who was throwing knives. But we caught some of them." Half a dozen men had been roped off so that they could not escape. "Going to call the cops, Mr. Ar?"

"Haven't they been around yet?"

"Nope."

"Then let's leave them out of it," decided Rollison. "I know most of the answers they could get. How much longer, Gabby?"

"Nearly finished, Mr. Ar, but you'll be very tender for a day or two. They had thick boots."

"I'll be careful," Rollison said. He waited until Gabby finished the massaging, and then began to sit up, cautiously; the pain wasn't as severe as he had expected, and soon he was on his feet. "I know we want Punchy Parks very badly indeed, Bill—he's the next best thing to Osgood."

Ebbutt said in a troubled voice: "Mr. Osgood would have to come a long way, Mr. Ar."

Rollison caught his breath.

"What does that mean?"

"The so-and-so's dead," Bill Ebbutt announced. "The doctors couldn't save him."

15

ARREST

Rollison walked along Gresham Terrace, at half past nine that night, alert to the possibility of the house being under police surveillance. If it were, Grice would put his men in the open, there would be no subterfuge. No one appeared to be watching, even the newspaper-men had given up. There was a light in the front room, so Jolly was home, and Sydney Bishop should be there, too. Rollison unlocked the street door, always necessary at night, and paused after closing it. There seemed no sound. He went quickly up the stairs, half prepared to see someone on the top landing, but no one was there.

A sense of oppression and of danger was very close, and in some ways it was worse because he did not yet know why he was so deeply involved.

Why *should* Punchy Parks want him dead?

He opened the front door of the flat, and stopped short, for Perdita was saying brightly:

"Of course he'll be all right, don't be such a pessimist, Jolly."

Jolly, clearly despondent, was halfway towards the door. He stopped short at sight of Rollison.

"Good *evening*, sir. I'm very glad to see you!"

"Didn't you expect to?" Rollison asked.

"Did you know that Osgood had died, sir?"

"Yes."

"There have been a great number of telephone calls since that news, some threatening to kill you," said Jolly flatly.

Perdita came hurrying from the big room.

"Richard, darling, how wonderful to see you! Jolly's such an old Job's comforter, he thought you were in

126

prison or something." She ran to Rollison and flung her arms round him. "I *knew* you would come back, I—— Richard! What's the matter?"

Rollison stood holding his breath against the pain of her embrace. She pulled herself free and stared up at him. Jolly moved forward quickly, as if to offer physical support.

"Are you all right, sir?"

"I got mixed up with some old boots," Rollison told them.

Now Perdita looked mystified.

"Old *boots?*" she echoed.

"Ease me gently to a chair and prop me up with cushions, and I will tell you all about it," Rollison said. "The most vulnerable section is round the ribs, my mouth didn't suffer." He moved to his large and luxuriously comfortable armchair and lowered himself gingerly. Perdita stood over him, a frown putting an unfamiliar touch of severity on her beauty. "Whisky and soda, Jolly," Rollison demanded. He beamed on Perdita, determined at all costs not to let her suspect he knew about "Phyllis Shaw."

She bent down and kissed him.

"You're not hurt badly, are you?"

"Not badly at all," Rollison said. "And I'm hungry."

"There is some cold game pie, sir, with salad," Jolly interpolated.

"Get it, and I'll tell you the story while I'm eating," said Rollison. "Where is Syd Bishop?"

"In the kitchen," Jolly said. "I told him to stay there."

"I'd like him to hear the story, too," said Rollison.

Soon, he had told them everything he wanted them to know, and it was surprising how little he kept back. Perdita, on a pouffe close to him, looked up without a change of expression throughout the telling. Jolly sat primly on an upright chair, and Syd Bishop sat astride another, leaning on the back, as if he was never really at home unless he were straddling a saddle. Every now and again he burst out with an expletive rather than a comment, and when Rollison described how Ebbutt's men came to the rescue, he jumped up as if he longed for a chance to do battle at that very moment.

When Rollison had finished, Perdita said in a subdued tone: "I don't think I'd like to live this life of excitement all the time. And you say you still don't know what it's all about?"

"Do we, Jolly?" murmured Rollison.

"We have some indications, sir."

"Come again!" Syd barked.

"When we have slept on all this we will be able to see it in clearer perspective," Jolly said solemnly.

"*Sleep?* Who wants to sleep?" Syd complained indignantly.

"You certainly need a good night's rest," Rollison told him. "Ebbutt has every man he can lay his hands on searching for Punchy Parks, and the police don't know about Parks yet. He's the key to it all."

"The punch-line!" Syd interpolated, and then roared with laughter. "Why don't I go and help Ebbutt?"

"I've a different job for you," Rollison said.

"Such as?"

"Go and see your sister," said Rollison quietly, "and ask her what she can tell us. Ask her whom she's in love with, too," he added gently. "Find out why she was frightened into lying about knowing me. You're much more likely to make her talk than I am—or even Mrs. Shortt. And she must talk soon, Syd, if she isn't to suffer the same fate as your father."

As the words sunk in, the room seemed to grow cold. Perdita gasped. Syd's excitement died away, and alarm and apprehension replaced it. Jolly was the only one who did not seem surprised.

"You mean she's in *danger?*" Perdita asked helplessly.

"Grave danger."

"Why the hell should she be?" demanded Syd, anger bursting through his fear.

"She lived at home and might well know what your father knew," said Rollison. "She worked at Ticky's, and will know how the other girls were persuaded to lie about my affray with Osgood. She was prevailed on to say I was her child's father—is she a natural liar, Syd?"

"She hates lying!"

"So probably strong pressure was used," said Rollison. "And because she knows what the pressure is, the other side in this affair will be alive to the danger that she might talk to the police. They'll want to stop her."

"But she's been moved to a nursing home with police protection!" Sydney Bishop cried. "If they can't look after her, who can?"

"If she hasn't told all she knows by the time she leaves she'll be in acute danger," Rollison insisted. "Go and make her talk, Syd. Once the truth is known, the police can act. We'll find the killer of your father and the man who betrayed your sister. Only *you* can do this. No one else can."

Slowly, heavily, Syd Bishop said: "I daresay you're right. Okay, I'll try."

When he had gone, Perdita rose slowly from the pouffe, looked closely at Rollison and asked:

"Do you *really* think she's in danger while she's with the police?"

"I think Syd is more likely to make her talk if he thinks she is."

"But surely he's confident that the police will look after her."

"He's been brought up to mistrust them and to have no faith in them," Rollison reasoned. "There are still far too many families in the East End who regard the police

129

as their natural enemies—if you've been brought up in that invironment the delusion stays with you all your life."

"Toff," said Perdita, "you're far too cunning. You ought to be a politician."

"But politicians can be honorable men," declared Rollison. "We need to know all that Betty Bishop can tell us, and this is the most likely way to find out."

"I could try."

"She would know you at once as a policewoman in disguise."

Perdita began to laugh, and as she did so a sound came from the street—a shout, more shouting, then the blast of a police whistle, loud and clear even at this distance up. Rollison started to spring from the chair, felt as if his ribs were breaking, and dropped back. Jolly appeared and crossed quickly to the window as Rollison eased himself forward. Perdita put an arm round him in support.

"Carefully, now," she said.

"What was that?"

"A police whistle."

"Do you think Sydney——" Perdita broke off.

"Yes," said Rollison shortly.

They reached the window, and Jolly stood aside without comment, although his eyes told a story he knew the Toff would not like. Perdita and Rollison looked down into the street.

On the other side, in clear view beneath a lamp, three men were struggling. One was Sydney Bishop, arms whirling furiously. Two more men were running across the road towards the group, but before they reached it, Syd broke free, turned and raced away. Rollison felt a curious mixture of emotions—lightheartedness for this boy's courage, depression because he had no chance.

"He'll make it!" Perdita cried. "Look!"

Syd was near a corner, and it really seemed that he had a chance, after all, but another man, appearing suddenly, dived for the youth's ankles. He brought Syd crashing down. Perdita flinched, and gasped:

"Can't you do *any*thing?"

"Not by helping him now," Rollison said. "It looks as if they came to arrest him, and he tried to get away."

Perdita was biting her underlip as she stared down, seeing two men lift Sydney up and carry him to a police car which was double-parked only a few yards away; the youth seemed to be unconscious. It was not until the car moved off that Perdita spoke.

"Richard—*you* don't think he could have killed his father, do you?"

"I don't think he did, but obviously he could have done so," answered Rollison. He moved cautiously towards the desk and the telephone, dialed Whitehall 1212, and when Scotland Yard answered, asked if Grice were there. While he was holding on, Perdita came hurrying across the room.

"I'd forgotten! They might arrest you, too!"

"Then there'll be only you and Jolly to carry on the fight," Rollison said drily. "Really want to help?"

"Desperately," Perdita said. "That boy——" She broke off. "How can I?"

"Yes, Rolly," Grice said into the telephone.

"Bill, there's been a fracas outside my flat—with young Bishop in the middle of it. Is he being charged?"

"Yes," said Grice. "We found the knife buried in the back garden of his house. It's his, his fingerprints were on it and a neighbor saw him go into the garden about five o'clock this morning. If you're still interested in him, send your solicitor round, otherwise he'll get legal aid from the courts."

"I'll call Ronnie Scott," Rollison said at once. "Are you in a mood to carry out a lot of arrests tonight?"

"Meaning, will I send and pick you up," Grice said. He sounded hard-voiced and almost hostile. "No—I can get you when I want to."

"Meaning, you know you couldn't hold me on the charge of causing Osgood's death," said Rollison.

"I shouldn't count on that."

"Bill," said Rollison reproachfully, "you're still not being very friendly."

"I don't feel very friendly."

"Pity. I want to ask you a favor," Rollison said.

There was a long pause, and in it Rollison felt his anger rising. His ribs hurt, he was irritated with Grice because of his continued hostility, he was annoyed with Perdita for having taken the flat in Circle Road, he was resentful that Sydney had been charged although he, Rollison, had been given no warning. It would have been very easy to let fly at the Yard man, and every moment of waiting was excoriating.

Grice said suddenly: "Sorry—someone came in. What favor?"

"I want Mrs. Shortt to go and visit Betty Bishop, and try to get her to talk."

"No reason why not," said Grice without any hesitation. "*We* can't make her talk, but we're pretty sure she knows a great deal, is only——" He broke off. "I'll tell the policewoman who's with the girl to leave Mrs. Shortt alone with her for half an hour. Will that do?"

"Thank you, Bill," said Rollison, humbly.

When he rang off, he felt better, and very glad he had not lost his temper with Grice.

He told Perdita, and in five minutes she was hurrying out of the flat with a scrap of paper in her hand bearing the name and address of the hospital. Rollison was telephoning the solicitors, arranging for one of the partners to go to Scotland Yard straight away.

As he replaced the receiver and the door shut behind Perdita, Rollison said: "She's rented one of Kate McGuire's flats, Jolly."

"Indeed, sir," said Jolly, and considered this piece of information. "I must admit to being puzzled by her attitude and her interest in the affair—or more correctly, in the *people* in the affair. If I may say so, sir, she appears to have a very affectionate disposition. She is obviously deeply concerned for young Bishop, for his sister, for the baby and"—Jolly coughed, a rare indication of nerves— "for you, sir."

"Is it real, or is it put on?" demanded Rollison.

"The affection? I *think* it is genuine—she seems to be an outstandingly warm-hearted young person." After a pause, Jolly went on: "I am more concerned for you, sir. If Parks is so desperately anxious to kill you, he is hardly likely to stop trying."

"No," said Rollison. "And if we should be wrong about Mrs. Shortt, she's in an ideal position to do a lot of harm. Jolly—why should Parks be so determined to kill me?"

"When was the first indication that he wished to do so, sir?" asked Jolly primly.

"Tonight, I suppose."

"After Osgood's death."

"Yes."

"Could his motive be revenge, sir?"

"That would leave us without a motive for trying to involve me in the baby business," Rollison objected. "Jolly—isn't this a case of the glaringly obvious?"

"In what way, sir?"

"Osgood and whoever worked with him, Punchy Parks among them, wanted to stop me from taking the action they expected me to take."

Jolly, expecting some crystal-clear revelation, looked slightly disappointed, even a little reproachful.

"Yes indeed, sir. But action about *what?*"

"There's the rub, we don't know," said Rollison, "but we're probably not seeing the wood for the trees. Grice is sour and wouldn't be so without a reason. Osgood tried to involve me in the baby business. Punchy Parks or someone we don't know swung the workers at Ticky's against me. Now Punchy is after my blood—if killing is the only way to stop me doing something he thinks I'm doing, or likely to do, he will kill me. Are you following my reasoning?"

"Very closely, sir," Jolly assured him.

"What I'm supposed to be doing has got under Grice's skin. We know that Grice suspected Osgood of organizing shop-lifting and bag-snatching and the smaller felonies. No, Grice appeared to think I was working against Osgood because of this. Is that what Osgood thought, and Punchy Parks thinks? That I'm investigating these organized crimes, and have found something that can incriminate them?"

Jolly paused, pondered and pronounced: "It is a most rational and obvious explanation, sir. They would certainly only attempt *murder* if they had good reason to believe you were a real threat to them."

"That could be why they murdered Mario Bishop, too, because he'd learned something which he could use to blackmail them. There's one obvious thing I did which might make them think I'm really close to their secret."

"Indeed, sir?"

"I went to Ticky's and kidnapped Osgood," Rollison said. "If there is shop-lifting and bag-snatching on a big scale, there have to be a lot of people involved. These are more likely to be women than men. There are a lot of women employees at Ticky's, and next door there are fancy goods and costume jewelry wholesalers. Don't you think it's time I paid another call on Ticky's?"

16

PERDITA'S RAGE

There was a strong case for another visit to Ticky's, Jolly agreed, but a stronger one for suggesting that the police should carry out such a visit. In that way, Jolly reasoned, Rollison would be back in favor with Grice.

"And it is a great pity that your relationship is strained, sir, if I may say so."

"A very great pity," Rollison agreed. "But Grice can't act without *prima facie* evidence to justify a search warrant, whereas I can. We'll think about it."

"There is another thing to think about," Jolly said. "Personal protection, sir. I think the police should be informed of the attacks on you at Mallow's Club."

"Then Ebbutt and his boys will be on the spot," Rollison objected. "No, we won't tell the police. But we could ask him to let us have a couple of men back and front, until the alarm is over."

"I'll do that at once," Jolly said with alacrity. "Is there anything I can do for your bruises?"

"Not until the morning," Rollison answered. "Gabby's given a list of instructions to make me as good as new."

"I am of the opinion that I can work on my own initiative, sir, without the benefit of gratuitous advice."

Obviously Jolly was put out; and a put-out Jolly was always a reflection of a worried Jolly. Rollison did nothing to reassure or soothe him, and he poured Rollison a brandy then went off to his own quarters, to telephone Ebbutt, and doubtless devise other methods by which he could protect his employer. Rollison sat back to reflect, and found himself dozing; the excitements and the physical exertion of the day culminating in the battering at Mallow's, had been a bigger strain than he cared to admit. The brandy warmed and soothed, taking fears away, but also taking away acuteness and lucidity of thought.

He felt sure he was right about Ticky's, was vaguely aware that there were still some factors not explained. Mental images swam hazily before him, of the baby, Betty Bishop, Punchy Parks and the knife-thrower, Osgood, Syd Bishop—and an ugly red gash across a lean throat . . .

He dropped off into more than a doze; soon it was a deep sleep . . .

He heard noises through this sleep.

His first conscious thought was that it was morning; that the banging and battering on the door heralded Syd Bishop. He soon realized that something very unusual was taking place.

Jolly was raising his voice.

"*You are not to disturb him, Madam!*"

"I *must* see Mr. Rollison." That was Perdita, her voice high and shrill, obviously she was in one of her fiery moods.

"I will not allow you to disturb him." Jolly was as angry, which was astonishing.

"If you don't let me pass, I'll——"

"Madam," said Jolly, now in a cold rage, "I must insist that you leave."

Rollison opened his eyes a fraction and saw the pair standing in the doorway leading from the hall, Jolly slightly ahead of Perdita, and blocking her path. Her hands were raised, her eyes sparked magnificently.

"Get—out—of—my—way!" She ejaculated each word as if it were a bullet.

There would be a real conflict if this went on, so Rollison divined, and emitted a tactful snore, shifting heavily in his chair. Each of the others looked towards him quickly.

"He's awake!" cried Perdita.

136

"He is not. Madam, will you please——"

"What's happening?" Rollison muttered, opening his eyes as if from deep sleep. "Oh, hallo, hallo. You back, Perdita? I must have dropped off."

Jolly, defeated, stood aside; his face was pale and his anger showed by the tightening of his lips. Perdita surged past him, and it was easy to imagine that she would hurl herself at Rollison.

"Hey!" exclaimed Rollison in genuine alarm. "What is it this time?"

"You *beast!*" Perdita cried furiously. "You deceitful *beast!* I *hate* you. And *you're* the man I thought was going to be honest with me, the man I trusted."

By now, and with caution, Rollison was sitting upright.

"I am not a beast," he denied defensively.

"Mr. Rollison," Jolly put in with almost painful politeness, "I really think that Mrs. Shortt should be restrained."

"Restrained!" She spun round on him. "You're as bad as he is."

"Sir," Jolly said, now pale with rage, "I must protest."

"I protest with you," Rollison said, poker-faced. "Perdita, accuse me if you must, but leave my manservant alone, he is never guilty. Calm down and tell me what's upset you."

"*You* know what's upset me, you——"

"I can guess, but I don't know," Rollison said. "Tell me."

As he spoke, he felt a strange weight of depression, almost of gloom. He knew quite well what she was going to say, of course, there could be no serious doubt, yet he could hardly believe it possible. He knew that Jolly, still incensed, was just as aware of what was coming as he was.

"You *are* the baby's father!" Perdita cried. "Poor Betty told me so. And—and you wouldn't admit it, you
137

left her to fend for herself, you didn't even give her any money."

Rollison sat still.

Jolly said *sotto voce*: "This is quite unforgiveable."

"Unforgiveable!" echoed Perdita, "It's despicable."

"Jolly," Rollison said, "why do you think she should lie?"

"I'm not lying."

"Exactly when a lie ceases to be a lie and becomes a mere untruth is a moot point we must thrash out one day when we have more time. In this instance I was, of course, referring to Betty," Rollison said dispassionately.

"She could be frightened into lying." Jolly made a great effort to regain his composure. "There has been much talk of blackmail and pressure brought to bear in this case."

"Oh, don't try to keep that up!"

"There's another possible explanation," Rollison went on suavely. "To shield the real father."

"Of *course*, sir," Jolly said, as if responding to a revelation.

"Who on earth would she want to shield?" Perdita would not be ignored.

"That's what we need to find out," said Rollison. "There always were two possible explanations of the lie, if she actually uttered it. Fear of blackmail, and fear that she would harm someone whom she loved."

After a moment's silence, Perdita said in a slightly milder voice:

"That's what you said before, when you asked me to find out whom she loved."

"Yes," said Rollison.

"You mean you seriously think she's shielding someone."

"If she isn't being blackmailed. How was she, Perdita?"

Slowly, thoughtfully Perdita answered: "Well—very

138

overwrought." She moistened her lips, glanced at Jolly, and appeared to be almost shame-faced. "As a matter of fact, when she first said it was you I couldn't believe it. I was very stern with her, and said how wicked it was to accuse a man who was doing so much for her and her brother. Then she got excited—terribly excited, almost hysterical. She swore it was you. Anyhow," Perdita added with a new spark of defiance, "she convinced me completely at the time, but oh, heavens, who *am* I to believe?"

"Me," said Rollison.

"I'm not so sure. But I have to admit that she behaved almost as if she was really frightened, and if she was shielding someone, that would explain her fear, I suppose." Perdita moved towards the desk and studied the Trophy Wall. "I am sorry I lost my temper, Jolly," she said airily.

"You are very gracious, Madam. If I in any way——"

Before he could finish what was doubtless going to be a most punctilious and formal apology, the telephone bell rang. Jolly picked up the receiver. A moment later, he said:

"Mr. Scott, sir."

"I'll take it," said Rollison. He levered himself out of his chair and moved cautiously to the desk. "Hallo, Scotty . . . Sure? . . . Yes, most unfortunate . . . No, I don't think there's a ghost of a chance of getting bail . . . I'll be there if I can . . . Does Bishop understand I still don't believe he did it? . . . Good . . . One other thing, Scotty . . . You still there? . . . Good. Find out from him if his sister had a particular boyfriend, anyone she might be shielding . . . Eh? . . . Be your age, man—a boyfriend, the child's father . . . But don't let young Bishop know what you're driving at or he will probably try to break your neck . . . Thanks . . . Good night."

Rollison replaced the receiver, and said very thoughtfully:

"Syd will be formally charged at the East End Police Court tomorrow morning, and will almost certainly be remanded for eight days. I don't think we can afford to wait eight days, do you, Jolly?"

"I do not, sir." Jolly drew in a deep breath, and glanced at Perdita, back at Rollison, and finally spoke to Perdita in a voice which was almost an appeal. "Mrs. Shortt, in my opinion it is most advisable to inform the police of the attack by the man Parks; once the police are searching for him there will be much less danger for Mr. Rollison, who is in no condition to take further risks. Don't you agree, Madam?"

Jolly had so far forgiven her as to plead with her to join forces with him against Rollison.

"It's the only possible thing to do," Perdita said promptly.

"You see, sir." Jolly's eyes were positively beseeching.

"Well, I'm not going to," said Rollison flatly. "We've still another card to play which the police can't possibly use. I mean, Kate McGuire. There's a sound chance that Punchy Parks is hiding at her place, and I want to check on that, tonight. What we really need is someone who can search the house without being suspected, it should be easy to find out if a man's in one of her flatlets. We'd better ask Bill Ebbutt if the wife or the girl-friend of one of his men will take a chance. Gabby has a daughter who has a judo black belt, I believe."

Jolly, obviously, had taken his cue.

"It is a very risky thing for a woman, sir."

"Don't I know it. But riskier for a man." He frowned as he stared at Jolly, deliberately avoiding Perdita's eyes. "I wonder if I ought to call Bill Ebbutt and see if Gabby's daughter will play."

Perdita kept looking from one to the other, as if watching a game of ping-pong, and not wishing to miss anything. Two or three times she opened her mouth as if to comment, but each time closed it again.

Into the pause which followed Rollison's last words, she said in a quiet, very circumspect voice:

"Why don't you ask me?"

"You!" ejaculated Rollison. "Don't be silly."

"Really, Madam," Jolly protested, and nearly added: "*Tcha-tcha*."

"Don't look at me as if I were a half-wit or a jellyfish," said Perdita in vexation. "I am quite capable of searching the house, and of looking after myself. And I have certain other advantages, too."

"Now, come——" Rollison began.

"We do appreciate——" Jolly temporised.

Perdita opened her handbag, and from it took two keys, which she held out on the palm of her hand so that each man could see.

"Advantages which include a key to the street door, and a key to the flats," she announced. "When I heard where Betty had been found, I thought it would be a good thing to have a foot in the enemy's camp." She smiled with deep satisfaction, looking from one to the other. "So it isn't a question of which woman you will ask. It's simply a question of deciding *when* I'll start. Forget Gabby's daughter."

Perdita was as honest as the day was long, thought Rollison.

Of course it remained just possible that she had told him of this as part of a deeply laid plan to win his confidence, but he accepted the possibility without believing in it. Perdita was as guileless as a child.

And she was right: she alone had a reasonable chance of finding out whether Punchy Parks was at Kate McGuire's house, and of getting in and out without raising an alarm. There was one weakness, one spot in which she was extremely vulnerable.

Parks had seen her and so would recognize her.

How could she be allowed to take such a risk?

17

PERDITA'S RISK

Perdita waited without speaking for what must have seemed a long time, then gave a sigh of exasperation and swung round to the Trophy Wall. There were all the weapons in neat array, from pistols to knives, from coshes to spanners, from swords to daggers; one could take one's choice. Her choice appeared to be a small pearl-handled revolver, used many years ago by an Italian adventuress who had hoped to part the Toff from his money. This pistol was suspended from a tiny silvered bracket by the trigger loop, and Perdita took it down carefully, turned, held it out towards Rollison and asked with spurious non-chalance.

"May I borrow this?"

"No," said Rollison. "There aren't any bullets for it. Are you really serious?"

"You should know me well enough by now to realize when I'm serious."

"Have you really thought, or is this another of your generous impulses."

"I don't know about my generous impulses, but I do know that since the beginning of this affair, I've wanted to *do* something. Just this once. I'd hate to live this dangerously all the time, but now—well, I suppose it's a kind of fatalism. It is *not* a habit of mine to repair to a Mayfair apartment with a handsome bachelor, and I can't imagine what made me do it, but having come—well, it *did* seem like fate. As if I had to be involved in that baby's future, and you must admit that its future is being decided now. It isn't that I feel terribly brave," went on Perdita with engaging frankness. "In fact, I feel weak at the knees at

142

the thought of it, but I'm obviously the one to go. You *will* make sure that help will be at hand, won't you?"

Jolly was staring at her as she spoke.

"Yes indeed, Madam," he said gently. "You can be quite sure I will."

"There's one thing you may not have realized," Rollison said.

"Go on—scare me some more."

"Kate McGuire might be for Punchy Parks or against him—we don't yet know. We need to."

"I can try to find out."

"I don't quite mean that," said Rollison. "If she's on his side, then she will have told him about you becoming a tenant, because she will have placed you from newspaper photographs. And if you go in alone—and you can't have anyone with you if you're going to do the job properly —there might not be any time to come to the rescue. I mean," he added with great deliberation, "they didn't waste any time with Syd's father."

Perdita lost color, and shivered. It was some time before she asked off-handedly:

"What weapon *can* I take, then?"

It was all Rollison could do to stop himself from moving across and hugging her. Jolly spread his hands, as if recognizing a kind of natural courage allied to integrity against which there could be no arguing. It was he who suggested:

"The palm gun, sir, perhaps."

"Undoubedly the palm gun," Rollison confirmed.

"I've heard of them," said Perdita. "What are they like?"

There was a tiny palm gun of Swiss manufacture, in a locked drawer in Rollison's wardrobe. He took it out from a miscellany of ingenious weapons and demonstrated it to her.

It was about the size of a man's wrist-watch, and one side was coated with an adhesive which would keep it

143

stuck to the centre of the palm of the hand. The other side was covered with esh-colored plastic. It had a tiny barrel like a watch-winder, close to the V caused when the third and middle fingers were separated. The gun was fired simply by closing the hand; the first squeeze released the safety-catch, the second fired the gun.

"But the bullets are so tiny," Perdita remarked.

"It will kill at short range," Rollison told her grimly. "If you should really be in danger, fire at the stomach or at the eyes."

Once again Perdita shivered.

"I see." She gave a strained little laugh. "Can I go soon? I shall lose all my courage if I don't."

"Yes," Rollison said. "Very soon. And Perdita—there will be men in the street and at the back of the house, you won't be left alone a moment longer than you have to. We need to learn those two things. Is Kate McGuire for or against Parks? And is Punchy Parks at the house?"

When Perdita had gone to get ready for the expedition, Jolly said soberly:

"Are you sure she should be allowed to go, sir?"

"There's no one else with the same chance."

"You would feel terrible if things went wrong, and she were to be killed—even injured."

"I would feel terrible," Rollison agreed soberly.

"Will you be there, sir?"

"Yes. She'll go by taxi. I'll be there ahead of her, and I'll arrange for Gabby's daughter Flo to be at hand; and for Ebbutt's men to be at Circle Road in strength. You follow Mrs. Shortt."

"I wish you were wholly fit," said Jolly, almost in anguish, then he straightened his shoulders and pulled himself up sharply. "I really don't know what is the matter with me over this affair, sir. I am continually allowing my emotions to overrule my intelligence and my

144

discretion. I am afraid I was most impertinent to Mrs. Shortt."

Rollison grinned.

"I know," he said. "I heard the uproar." He gripped Jolly's arm. "Perhaps we're getting wiser as we grow older, Jolly. Perhaps there's more room for emotion than we've allowed in the past. Look after her, won't you?"

"I will indeed, sir," Jolly promised.

Rollison arrived at Circle Road by taxi, and found Ebbutt, Gabby and Gabby's Flo already waiting. He knew Flo slightly. She was a slim, pretty and rather retiring blonde, a little overcome by the situation, but not even remotely afraid.

"Don't you worry about Flo," Gabby said. "They don't come any tougher."

Six of Ebbutt's men were at hand when Rollison saw Perdita arrive in a second taxi, and let herself in. His own heart was thumping, in spite of all reassurances.

He saw Jolly draw up in the little Austin, not far from Number 93; Jolly's heart would be thumping, too.

He saw Ebbutt's men, some in doorways, two in cars, one on a motor-cycle. Their hearts might also be thumping, but not for the same reason as were Rollison's and Jolly's.

It was a little after midnight, few people were about, cars were parked in almost unbroken line at either kerb. Heavy traffic on the main road rumbled and whined. The rain had stopped, but there was heavy cloud and the streets were still damp.

Rollison watched the house into which Perdita had gone.

Perdita had never known her knees feel so weak. Now that she was here she hated it, and yet nothing would have kept her away.

There was a good, bright light on in the hall. From

145

somewhere in the house there came the sound of music, not very loud; otherwise all was quiet. She crept to the door of Kate's room and listened, but heard nothing. She started stealthily up the stairs, then realized how absurd that was, as she had every right to be here, so squared her shoulders and walked up briskly. She unlocked the door of her own room—then caught her breath.

She heard a *snore*.

Her heart beat like a trip hammer, and she was close to panic, but did not move. When she felt steadier she opened the door an inch or two, muscles flexed, already to slam it closed again, and race down the stairs. She heard nothing for a moment, but the snore came again—from the room on the other side of the landing.

She groped for the light in her own room, pressed down the switch and pushed the door open. Everything was exactly as she had left it, giving the same shiny, newly decorated impression as the rest of the house. She went inside and closed the door, trembling. She was a fool! She should never have volunteered to come here. Why, she had demanded the "privilege;" *Privilege!*

She touched the gun in her right hand; it did not seem real, *nothing* seemed real. But there was that snoring sound.

Women sometimes snored. She couldn't be sure this was a man.

The only way to check was by looking in. Stealthily, her heart beating very fast, she approached the door from behind which the sounds were coming. Slowly, slowly, she turned the handle and pushed. Nothing happened. A miscellany of information on key-holes flitted confusedly through her mind, and stooping down, she looked through this one. A bright, pinpoint of light met her eye. No key, then. A bolt. Frustrated in this, her first essay into detection, shown to be miserably ill-equipped for it, she moved back to the window of her own flat.

Jolly sat at the wheel of the Austin, Rollison next to him. Reassurance swept over her.

If she could only look into the window of the opposite room.

She couldn't, but surely these friends of Rollison could!

She opened her bedroom door and went downstairs very quietly, opened the street door and stepped down to the pavement. Almost at once, Jolly appeared, and there was urgency in his voice.

"Can I help, Madam?"

Bless Jolly!

"Someone's snoring in the back room on the first landing, near the fire escape," Perdita whispered. "I don't know whether it's a man or a woman."

"We will find out," Jolly said. "Is there anything else?"

"Not yet," Perdita said. "I just wanted you to know that."

She gave an impression of almost careless confidence, but the moment the street door was closed behind her, all her fears surged back. She stood looking up at the light shining from her own room, heard the music and the snoring, and realized that the music was coming from Kate McGuire's apartment, and not from upstairs. It hadn't stopped. She went closer to Kate's door and listened intently, feeling sure this was from a long-playing record, old-fashioned Palm Court light orchestral music.

She pushed at the door, and almost cried out in surprise, because it yielded. Why wasn't it locked? She pushed it wider and the music sounded clearer. She stepped inside. On the right was a closed door, in front of her was the kitchen; the music was coming from the closed room. She tried that door, too, and like the other, it opened. She pushed it wider.

Faint light came from a window at the back of the house.

She heard only the music, which seemed to come from the top of a wardrobe heavily shadowed against the pale wall. She discerned the shape of the bed, and Kate McGuire's dark head on it. As her eyes became accustomed to the gloom, she saw that one arm was outside the bedclothes, and the other covered.

Then she saw the dark streak across the woman's throat.

At first, an awful constriction caught her own throat, she felt as if she were choking, and her breath wouldn't come. A strange pain, bringing icy coldness, spread through her limbs, invading her whole body; she remembered her mocking comment to Rollison as he had lifted her over the threshold of his flat. They had pitched forward, staggering—and it seemed as if they had been staggering ever since, and that there was still no certainty that they wouldn't fall.

The recollection vanished. Panic took its place. She opened her mouth to scream, knowing it would bring some relief, but suddenly she thought:

"That won't help!"

If the man Parks were upstairs, he would hear, and so would others in the house. She remembered Rollison describing the way in which he had told the police about Bishop's murder; no fuss, nothing to raise an alarm. That was what she must do.

Then she wondered: *am* I right?

She drew closer to the bed, staring until abruptly she retched, and then swung round, ice-cold and shivering. She reached the door and clung to it for some seconds, trying to control her body, but when at last she reached the porch again, she was still trembling.

This time, Rollison was at hand. He sensed something was badly wrong, and put an arm about her, then held both her hands in one of his.

"What is it, Perdita?"

She tried to answer. "K-K-K-Kate is——"

148

Jolly came up, and a young woman—Gabby's Flo.

"Look after Mrs. Shortt, Jolly," Rollison said. "Take her to the car." He supported her until Jolly and Flo took over, and another man whom she did not recognize joined him. Though a sense of horror persisted, it was shot now by a feeling that everything would be all right, and that danger was over and she could relax. But when she was sitting next to the girl in the back of the car, she began to tremble violently again. Being soothed by Jolly was like being soothed by a benevolent uncle. There was some quality of human understanding in both him and Rollison.

The Toff——

She felt that she was only just beginning to understand what manner of man he was.

Rollison stood over the body of Kate McGuire.

In that moment he felt that he hated himself. But for him, this woman might still be alive.

He knew, in fact, that he was flagellating himself unjustly, for there was little more he could have done. He had sensed that she was in danger, but there had been no certainty. Recalling the throbbing vitality of the body that now lay so still, remembering the flashing, storming brilliance of the eyes now closed in death, he began to suspect the explanation of one most puzzling thing.

She had probably brought him into this affair, because of fears that she and others were in danger which by herself she could not face.

He felt that he was as right in this supposition as if it had been written in front of him in letters a foot high.

She lay on her back exactly as Mario Bishop had lain. She must have been drugged, or in a heavy sleep; she had made no attempt to defend herself. It looked almost as if the same knife had been used.

That thought changed his mood, and started him thinking logically again. It could not be the same knife, since the police had the one which had killed Syd's father. And this time the killer could not have been Syd. The second murder would give Grice a jolt; it was time something jolted Grice in this affair.

He thought of the knife-thrower—the dark-skinned man.

He must call the police, but first he must look round. There might be some clue which held more significance for him than for them. He scrutinized the top of the bed, looked underneath it and around the room, but there was nothing; the killer appeared to have stepped straight in, done his foul deed and left without a trace.

The room did not seem to have been searched.

Rollison looked quickly but thoroughly through the dressing-table drawers, the wardrobe, a tall-boy, a vanity case, a travel case, a writing case. It was in this that he had his second shock—one that struck sharply, yet made him tremendously glad that he had searched before sending for the police.

There was a sealed envelope, addressed to:

Richard Rollison—The Toff
To be opened only after my death.

And in brackets beneath this, a sentence which was characteristic of the woman:

(If no one kills me first, I'll tell him all about it.)

18

COLD RIVER

Rollison's hand was at his pocket to take out a penknife and slit the envelope open, but he stayed the movement for two reasons. There was a sound outside; and he realised that he could not delay calling the police long enough to read the contents.

He turned to the door, and Gabby.

"Everything okay, Mr. Ar?"

"No, Gabby, but it will be. What have you got for me?"

"That room Jolly asked Flo to take a dekko at—it's a woman snoring! Couldn't do better myself!" That appealed enormously to Gabby's sense of humor. "There's no man around in the back rooms."

"Good," said Rollison. "I don't think we'll need you any more, I'm going to send for the police. You and the boys had better make yourselves scarce here—and go on to Houndsditch."

"Ebby told us to go there when you'd finished, Mr. Ar. You coming along yourself?"

"Soon," Rollison said.

"Okay," said Gabby. He turned away, then swung back on his heel. "There's something I forgot to tell you. Old Ebby said the police had been around inquiring for Rube. They wanted to know if he'd had a chance of conking Osgood. He had plenty of chance all right. Looks as if you're in the clear over that, Mr. Ar."

"Fine. Thank Bill for me."

"Sure will. And there's another thing. He said he'd got some of the addresses of those women at Ticky's. Do you want them now?"

"If I need them, the morning will do," Rollison said.

He did not believe he would need them now; the things he had wanted to learn from those women who had changed their tune would probably be in the sealed envelope. This was just small enough to tuck into his inside breast pocket. He turned to the telephone and dialed Whitehall 1212—getting the Yard's telephone exchange, not the *Information Room*. He said simply:

"This is Richard Rollison. Tell Mr. Grice or whoever is acting for him to send a Murder Squad to 93 Circle Road, Camberwell."

"Just one moment, please——"

Rollison rang off and went out, closing but not attempting to latch the door, which he noted had been forced. He walked briskly to the end of the street, and saw a bus coming from the South; by sprinting, he just caught it. He went up to the top deck, sat right at the front, and lit a cigarette. It was not often he felt as badly shaken as he was over this last fatality.

He blamed himself bitterly for Kate McGuire's death. It was no use saying that the police should have been watching her, or excusing himself because he hadn't been sure whose side she was on. He should have made sure she couldn't be killed, even used one of Ebbutt's men, if only to watch the flat. It was a matter for self-contempt that he had been sleeping—*sleeping*—in his armchair when that awful slash had killed her.

What had Grice said? And Jolly had echoed? That he wasn't himself in this case, he wasn't even seeing the obvious. The obvious had been that because she knew a great deal, Kate was as likely a victim as she was a suspect. He hadn't treated her seriously enough, hadn't acted fast enough.

Yet—could he have acted faster?

"Waterloo only," a Jamaican conductor said, when he took Rollison's fare.

Rollison got off outside the station, where he could get a taxi without trouble, but instead, he decided to walk over Waterloo Bridge. His ribs and shoulders were still painful, but he was now able to move with fair freedom. The Shell building was floodlit, but the lighting at the London County Hall and on St. Paul's, Big Ben and the Houses of Parliament, was out. Stars were shining now, but the wind was cutting across the river. He reflected on a dozen things. Perdita would be all right, Jolly would see to that. If he, Rollison, went to his flat, the police might be there—but before he went to Houndsditch he must read that letter from Kate. Where should he go? His club? That was in the West End, and here he was nearer the East End, where eventually he wanted to be. No restaurant would be open. But he could walk round to the Savoy Hotel and sit in the foyer—or, better still, the Strand Palace, where he was much less likely to be recognized.

As he decided to do this he felt better.

He was near the Strand side of the Bridge, close to the Embankment, and glanced down at the smooth surface of the river and the reflection of the stars. Most of the traffic was going in the other direction, away from the heart of the City, but quite a lot was behind him.

He did not notice the car which slowed down.

Two motor-cyclists roared past, reminding him of Sydney Bishop, and he watched their tail-lights, fiery beacons disappearing towards the Strand. He actually felt a hand on his arm before hearing a sound, and swung round.

A cosh smashed on to the side of his head.

The blow did not knock him out, but it dazed him. He was helpless, just aware of what was going on but quite unable to resist. There were three men—each powerful. One hooked his legs from under him, the others saved him from falling, and held him between them. He could hear the scraping of their feet on the paving-stones, and the harshness of their breathing; and he could see the baleful reflection of light in their eyes.

They hoisted him high.

They were going to toss him over.

He thought he heard a squeal of brakes, and some shouting, but could not be sure. He felt the rush of air as the two men hurled him sideways and let him go. He sailed over the railings of the bridge, clearing the top easily. He felt himself beginning to fall. The air whistled past his ears. His body was in excruciating pain, but he had the sense to know that he must protect his head before he hit the water.

He *might* smash on to a boat, or even one of the pillars of the bridge.

He managed to raise his arms and protect his head, before striking the river's surface, almost horizontally. It was icy cold, and on the instant he was numbed, and yet a great fear stabbed through him. If he lost consciousness, he would drown.

He held his breath.

The stunning effect of the impact was lessened by his realization of the danger, and his consequent stillness. He must let himself sink, let himself rise, then start to swim. Thank God that blow from the cosh hadn't knocked him out. He felt himself rising, and broke water. The first attempt at swimming brought such pain to his chest that he gasped and went under again, and this time found himself kicking out. *He must stop that!* He floated, turning slowly on to his back. He couldn't be far from the bank. Was the tide in or out? The south side seemed a long way off, the lights on the Embankment gleaming like jewels.

Suddenly the beam of a torch shone from the bridge, striking the water only a few feet away. Alarm flared in his mind; were his assailants looking for him—and if so, were they armed? He remembered the dark-skinned man, remembering his knives, the deadly accuracy of his aim.

But there were no knives, no bullets, only the lapping

154

water and the sound of a voice, several voices, shouting. Rollison attempted to strike out again, then he heard a terrific splash, and at the same moment the beam of light struck across his eyes. As it moved away it shone on the head of a man swimming strongly towards him.

"On your back!" this man ordered.

He attempted to answer, but no words came.

"Get on your back, I'll take you in."

He was right; the sensible thing for Rollison to do was to turn over on his back and allow himself to be drawn towards the bank. The man's voice had a familiar ring, but Rollison could not place it. He turned over slowly, the other slid into the life-saving position, and began to swim as if this was a daily practice for him.

They had not gone far before the stuttering roar of an engine sounded, throbbing harsh and loud over the water. Soon, a boat drew close, uniformed figures showed at the side, and Rollison felt a tug as a boat-hook jagged the shoulder of his coat; in minutes, he was on board, shivering, teeth chattering.

This was a police launch, of course.

And his rescuer was Gabby the Trainer.

"Sure you're all right, sir?" asked a River Division police sergeant.

"I'm fine. Warm as toast."

"Soon have you home."

"Yes. Thanks."

"Owe your friend here plenty."

"I do indeed."

"Like us to keep your clothes until they're dry?"

"No," Rollison said, almost too sharply. He wanted Kate's letter. "No, I'll take them. You'll see that Mr. Grice hears about this tonight."

"Yes, sir, don't worry."

Rollison, wrapped in a policeman's dressing-gown, and with his wet clothes in a sack, got into a police car, with

155

Gabby, who had stripped to singlet and trunks before diving in, but who was now fully dressed in trousers and sweater. He had told the police he had seen the attack and the way Rollison had been tossed over.

"Got me Life Saving Gold Medal years ago," he had announced. "It wasn't no trouble at all. Only pity of it is that the three baskets got away." He had already told the police that he had not recognized the men, and that his motor-cyclist "pal" had gone after the M.G. sports car which the assailants had used.

He had been riding his motor-cycle, when the assault had started. Now, Rollison realized that the two motor-cyclists had been Ebbutt's men, keeping an eye on him. Thank God they had! He sat next to Gabby, saying very little, warmed by a hot shower and two whiskies. They turned at last into Gresham Terrace, which was deserted, at least there were no newspapermen to make a song and dance over this.

"Come up and have a drink," Rollison said to Gabby.

"No thank you, sir," Gabby said. "You've got me address." He wrung Rollison's hand fervently. "The police driver will see me all right, sir, and I'll pick me bike up in the morning." He grinned. "Be a treat to go and get it from the garage at Scotland Yard."

Rollison smiled.

He let himself into the house, carrying the sack of clothes, and walked up the stairs with a great effort. But it was not until he approached the landing outside his flat that reaction really set in, and now he felt he hardly had the strength to grope for his key. He would have to open the sack and fumble inside the wet jacket to find it. But there was, after all, no need, for as he reached the top step the door opened and Jolly appeared.

For an instant the blandness, the imperturbability of Jolly's countenance changed to astonishment at the sight of the always so exquisitely groomed Rollison wearing a woollen dressing-gown two sizes too large for him and carrying a canvas sack. But for an instant only.

Twenty minutes later, Rollison was sitting up in bed. Opening Kate McGuire's letter with a paperknife, he began to read.

19

"HI, POP!"

There were several sheets of good quality paper, pale blue in color, and although they were wet, Kate's writing still showed firm and precise. Lucky she used waterproof ink, thought Rollison, as he peeled the damp sheets apart. The salutation was exactly what he might have expected.

"*Hi, Pop!*" she began . . . and a few lines farther down, she went on, ". . . *and you ought to be if you're not, no man like you should be childless, we need more of your kind in the world, not fewer. . . .*

"*In case you think this is a fan letter or something, don't make any mistake, I want you to do something for me—and for a lot of people. It didn't work out the way I expected. I thought when I brought the brat along it would start the ball rolling, but I didn't think it would roll so fast and so far.*"

Rollison looked up from the letter. It was some time since he had suspected she had brought the baby here, but he had never expected such a positive admission. Much that he should have found obvious was now falling into place. She had cared for Betty Bishop, seen her through her labor, brought the baby here wrapped in old clothes to create the foundling effect—and later, when Betty had seemed in danger, it was Kate who had telephoned the police, telling them where to find the girl.

The obvious things which had been so obscure. . . .

He read on:

"*I meant to come and see you, and do a deal—the truth to the newspapers about the child, in return for help for a lot of people.*"

Rollison thought almost passionately: Why the *hell*

didn't she come straight out and tell me? If only she had——

"*But Osgood and Parks were watching me. Don't get me wrong, Toff. I wanted to make sure the kid was safe, I knew you would look after it, it was just to whet your appetite for the big affair. They didn't know where Betty was but they knew I'd been keeping an eye on her. When I brought the kid to you they thought I'd told you all the rest, but I was too scared to wait, I knew they were on my heels. I should have told, but there wasn't a chance. Anyway, I was scared they'd find Betty if I didn't get back.*

"*That's right, Toff. I was scared. You don't know what it's like to be scared, do you?*"

Rollison thought: "So I don't know."

What kind of a reputation had he won for himself? Mr. Cold Blood?

"*I've been scared for a long time,*" the letter went on. "*Ever since I let myself get mixed up in this bloody business. Oh yes. I'm in it. I'm as guilty as hell. In the beginning it seemed so easy—a bloody good idea. I liked Ossy, then, I didn't know what he really was. Everything bad, that was Ossy. Corrupt. But lifting a few handbags and selling them to the girls—that seemed to be doing them a good turn. I didn't realize that Ossy was turning me into a fence—a Fence, Toff, Capital F!*"

Yes it was all so obvious, now.

"*It wasn't long before Ossy got the girls doing a bit of shop-lifting, too. He was a clever swine, never let anyone do too many jobs close together. But gradually everyone got into the habit of it. A kind of Union, it was—no one could work in that Machinists' Room if they weren't in the racket. It got so that if anyone didn't bring enough stuff in, Ossy put the fear of God into them. He'd use Punchy Parks, or some of the men from Mallows. Sometimes he'd beat them up, or use a razor on their faces, or threaten to tell their husbands they'd been laying with*

159

*other men. Anything to keep up the pressure. He made a
dossier on each one, the jobs they'd done, what they'd
been paid—everything to make them feel sure they'd be
found guilty if the police got on to them. No one dared
say anything. If any of the girls did have a little affair on
the side, he'd put that down, too. It was a reign of terror
at Ticky's, has been for years."*

Rollison pictured the way Osgood had sat up on his
platform, the way he had looked up when a woman at
one of the machines had paused for a moment. Yes—a
reign of terror was the right phrase.

"That day you came to Ticky's," the letter went on.
*"It was like a miracle. Someone turning on Ossy! At first
the girls couldn't believe it, but when they did—oh, my!
Were you the hero? And I pretended to be on your side
—at heart I was, Toff—but I was one of the leaders, see.
When you'd taken Ossy away, Punchy Parks took over—
told the girls he'd show the police those dossiers, saying
what they'd been doing, if they didn't say you had attacked Ossy, not the other way around. And I went
along with him, because I was scared for all the others
and for Betty.*

*"It was all beyond me by then, you see. You can see,
I'm sure of that. I just had to hope you could put one
across them. When Ossy got his and died, I thought you
were sure to be charged, that you wouldn't have a
chance to help. So I had to go along with Punchy, that's
why I phoned and told him you'd been to see me here.
Once Betty was safe, it wasn't so bad.*

"The only thing, though———"

There was a break in the letter, and an ink mark which
suggested she had dropped her pen, either in surprise or
in alarm. When the letter went on, the writing had
changed, and was much less precise and clear than it had
been.

*"What I don't know for sure is, who killed Ossy. It
wasn't you, but—was it Punchy? Did he want to take*

over for good and all? He certainly wants to now. And if he does it'll just about finish me. Punchy never liked me. Ossy did, we got along fine until I discovered what he was really like, but Punchy—I once turned him down and he always thought he was God's gift to women. Never forgiven me, he hasn't.

"He hasn't forgiven Mario, either.

"I swear to God he killed Mario because of me. Mario was a drunken so-and-so, but he was a man once. And when Ossy started to work on little Betty, and made her start shoplifting, Mario blew his top. They'd have killed him if I hadn't stood up for him. After that they kept him quiet with a few bottles of whisky whenever he got difficult. I tried to stop him drinking, I'd have married the man if he'd ever been sober enough to get to the church. So Punchy killed him. Well, I think it was Punchy. It may have been a pal of his, a man named Singh. Singh's the caretaker at Ticky's, see. Don't let Singh fool you. He's a Pakistani and can talk the language, but he's as much a Cockney as I am.

"So there you are, Toff.

"I thought if you once got your teeth into this problem, you'd work it out. Maybe you will. Maybe I'll be able to tell you all this. I could have when you came to see me, but in case I don't get the chance, I'm going to post this to you.

"Listen! Those dossiers are in the safe in the caretaker's flat at Ticky's. It's an old safe, and the key's always under the tablecloth they keep over it.

"So long, Toff—Pop, I mean!

                                        Kate McG."

Rollison put the letter down and lay on his back, looking at the ceiling, and the intricate moulding in the corners. The flat was very quiet. Jolly was still up, but Perdita was asleep in the spare room—under sedation, Jolly

161

had said; sedatives and essential drugs were always kept at the flat.

"*So long, Toff—Pop, I mean!*"

What a woman she had been!

He heard a gentle tap at the door, one that would not have wakened him had he been asleep.

"Come in," he called.

Jolly appeared with a tray, an omelette and a selection of English cheese, beer and coffee. He paused for a moment when he saw Rollison's expression and the hard brightness of his eyes. Then he placed the tray on the bedside table and a smaller one in front of Rollison, who handed him the letter, and said:

"Read it, Jolly."

"I will be very glad to, sir."

"It answers most of our questions," Rollison went on. He looked at the omelette without enthusiasm, but beginning to eat, found his appetite surprisingly good. Jolly sat in a chair in the corner, reading in the light of a lamp which stood on a Sheraton chest-of-drawers. As he recovered from the effect of the letter, Rollison began to face up to the immediate situation. All was not over, Ebbutt's men were at Ticky's waiting for him, and although Gabby might report what had happened, they would not move until Rollison had given the word to disband. Parks, Rube and a man named Singh were in Ticky's—on the third floor, the dark-faced Singh was the caretaker.

Rollison could not allow Ebbutt's men to raid the place on their own; on the other hand, he had never felt less like making the effort necessary for such a raid—which might cause an even deeper rift with the police than the one which already existed. The risk of that was negligible compared with the risk of failing to get Parks, of course. He realized that Parks was little more than a shadowy figure, a man in profile with a husky voice and often with a timid manner; but there had been nothing timid about him at Mallow's Club.

What would he, Rollison, do in Parks's position?

Surely, with the club members to call on, he would have the sense to put a guard on Ticky's, and surely such a guard would soon notice and report the concentration of Ebbutt's men. And once Parks knew they were there and who they were, he would surely realize that Rollison was on his way.

Rollison finished eating, still undecided. A moment later Jolly put the letter down. Jolly did not speak immediately, but it was clear that he was deeply affected.

Rollison said with an effort: "We still don't know the father."

"I can imagine that Mrs. McGuire deliberately omitted to mention that, so as to tease you, sir."

"Yes. Jolly—what would *you* do in this man Parks's place?"

"If it were humanly possible, get out of the country," answered Jolly promptly. "He must surely know that he cannot escape the consequences of his crimes if he stays in England."

"Unless he thinks he's kept his secret by killing Mrs. McGuire."

"Surely he *can't* believe that he would get away with it, sir, unless——" Jolly caught his breath. "I think I see what you mean." His voice deepened to a low key, and there was great anxiety in it. "Parks may believe that if he can now kill you, he will have a chance of keeping his secret and retaining his hold on the women at Ticky's." Jolly moved close to the bed. "Is that why you have not named him to the police?"

"I suppose so," Rollison said. "Subconscious reasoning mostly."

"Then you should name him, at once." It was more a plea than a command. "The moment he knows the police

163

are searching for him he will realize that it will not help him to kill you."

Rollison said: "It won't work, Jolly."

"I'm sure I'm right, sir."

"You would be right if you were dealing with a man of normal intelligence," said Rollison. "Not with this one. If he knows the police are after him, he'll still try to kill me because he'll blame me for his predicament. There's only one real question. Shall I go after him or wait for him to come after me?"

"With police protection, there will be no need to decide," Jolly said. "*Please* let me finish, sir. I know how you feel. I know that it must be a terrible blow to your —to your pride, sir, to accept such help from the police in a case of this kind. God knows what risks you've taken before—and I've taken them, too. Mr. Rollison," Jolly said, drawing back and stretching out both his hands— "have you ever known me to refuse to help, even at the risk of my life, if I believed it essential?"

Rollison said gently: "Never, Jolly."

"Thank you, sir." Jolly's voice quivered with emotion. "And if it were essential for you to take risks this time, I would gladly share them with you. I would urge you to take them. But it is not essential. The police can catch Punchy Parks without help from you. There is nothing left for you to do—it's all done, sir. This letter gives the answer. It clears you of everything. At Camberwell, I was wholly with you. I hated allowing Mrs. Shortt to take such a risk, but I could see that she might well lead us to the solution, and save lives.

"But not now, sir. There can be only one reason for going on and taking further risks: a loss of—*forgive* me, sir," Jolly added, "I don't mean any offence—loss of pride. It would be the first case you ever started but did not finish yourself. That is true, isn't it? The first out of hundreds of cases. But there has to be a first. There has to be."

Rollison sat and looked up at him, and Jolly waited for

an answer. But none came, and he went on with an almost despairing note in his voice.

"If you were a hundred percent fit, sir, it might be different. You might reasonably say that if you were to catch this man you might save lives. But you're not fit. The very way you move proves it—why, you were in a state of physical exhaustion when you got home, you looked as if you couldn't walk another step. To make any further attempt would be disastrous." He paused, then added with anguish in his voice: "*Wouldn't* it, sir?"

"It could be," Rollison said quietly. "Yes, it could be. But I have to try."

"Oh *no*, sir." Jolly sounded as if the end of the world had come.

"I have to, Jolly."

"You—you don't have to prove yourself to anyone, sir."

"No," Rollison said, and his lips twisted. "Not even to myself. If it were only pride, or self-esteem, I would be with you. But there's much more than that at stake."

"You're deceiving yourself, sir."

"No," said Rollison. "There's a lot at stake. The reputation of a hundred or more men and women."

"But you don't know them. They're strangers."

"Strangers, yes," agreed Rollison. "You didn't see them, did you?"

Jolly said, startled:

"I don't understand you."

"I'm sure you don't. You read about these women in Kate McGuire's letter. How Osgood gradually drew them into his net, until each one became criminal."

"Yes, but——"

"I saw the way they hated and also the way they feared Osgood," Rollison went on. "And I know that Parks was able to twist the screw so hard that they turned against me, although they had once seen me as a kind of Sir Galahad. If the police catch Punchy Parks, what is the first thing he will do?"

Jolly didn't speak, but a new expression dawned in his eyes; a look of hopelessness, of defeat following the moment when he had believed that victory was within his grasp.

"He will squeal on all of the others," Rollison said. "And when the police get their names and addresses and the evidence Kate talks about, they'll have to act. They couldn't fail to make charges. We might spend a fortune trying to defend these people, claiming that they had to commit the crimes out of fear, but—who would believe it without clear-cut evidence? And even if they were found not guilty, what about these proofs of infidelity? Every one of those women could be ruined for life, Jolly. You can see that, can't you?"

Jolly didn't speak.

"You must see it," Rollison went on softly. "It's so obvious, Jolly. It's obvious now why Kate McGuire inveigled me into this. She believed I would understand the plight of those women, and fight for them. She was right, too."

Still Jolly didn't speak.

"The only problem is—how?" Rollison now sounded almost as if he were talking to himself. "The proof we want is at Ticky's. You can take it as read that Parks is there, expecting me. If I withdraw Bill Ebbutt's men, he'll think—I hope he'll think—that I've given up. That will be the time for me to have a go, won't it?"

Jolly's hands dropped slowly to his side, and he moved a pace back from the bed.

"Yes, sir," he said in a voice that was only just audible, and then he added: "That will be the time for us to have a go."

Us.

Rollison looked up into the troubled eyes of his friend. His own were serene and confident, freer from anxiety than they had been for what seemed a long, long time.

"You've often been my hands and eyes, but this is the

first time you've ever been my ribs," he said. "Now, let's start thinking. We know that Punchy is at the factory, probably in the flat. We know he'll be expecting me, so we've got to give him something he doesn't expect. Jolly, we've got to go back to the early days. I need an old suit, a choker, my cloth cap——"

"Forgive me, sir," said Jolly, "but I think you would be more successful if you were to go as a youth on a motor-cycle. We can obtain jeans and a shiny jacket, and . . ."

The Toff's eyes began to glisten. . . .

Parks, and two men, were in the caretaker's flat above Ticky's. One of the men was the dark-skinned man who had nearly killed Rollison with his knives, the other was Rube.

All three saw Ebbutt's men move off, as Rollison had predicted, until at last, in those cold morning hours, the street was deserted.

"If he's coming, he'll come soon," Parks said. "I know how Rollison's mind works. He's so obvious. Must do everything himself—no one can be as good as the Toff. The bloody fool!"

He began to laugh, not wholly with amusement.

"I think we ought to get out," Rube muttered. "We ought to take those papers out of the safe, and lie low a bit."

"While Rollison's alive we can't lie low," said Parks. "That's the long and the short of it. When we've fixed him, we'll be in the clear. We don't have the police to worry about, while Rollison's around. He'll want to fix us himself. Got your knives ready, Singh?"

"All ready," said the Pakistani.

He had four throwing knives spread out in front of him, and the open window.

20

THE KNIVES

"Who's that?" asked Parks.

"That's not him," said Rube.

"Take it easy," Parks said to Singh. "It's a kid."

"Bit late, ain't he?" demanded Singh.

The motor-cycle which had turned into the street had stopped moving, but the engine stuttered and roared. The "youth" sat astride it, an easy target for Singh, being less than thirty feet away. Now and again the rider turned round in his saddle, as if he were expecting someone else.

"Why can't he stop his engine?" Rube grumbled. "Enough to wake the dead, that is. And the stink's awful!"

"What's he after?" asked Singh, nervously.

Then all three of them chuckled, for a girl turned the corner, walking quickly, hurriedly, towards the cyclist, who swivelled round in his seat and waited for her. Only when she drew up did he stop the engine and get off the saddle. In a moment they were hugging each other, and after a few seconds they moved towards the doorway a little farther along.

"Why don't we offer them a bed?" Rube muttered, and gave a nervous giggle.

"If they stay too long we've got to do something about it," Singh said.

"I'm going to have a drink," decided Parks. He laughed on a harsh note, and picked up a whisky bottle which stood on top of the safe where the dossiers were kept.

"All right?" whispered Rollison to Gabby's Flo.

"I'm okay," Flo said. "Tell me what to do again."

Rollison still had an arm round her waist in the doorway of the shop premises next to Ticky's. He wore a shiny leather jacket with a skull and crossbones in luminous paint, jeans which were a little too tight for him, cowboy boots and a wig; to anyone who saw him he was a youth who would mix with any long-haired mob. He carried a knife in his belt, and a small revolver; as well as a trick knife fastened to his forearm. He had used such weapons for many years, but what he most wanted was those dossiers, not a fight.

His chief anxiety now was the painful stiffness of his ribs, but that was easier than it had been.

"You wait until I've had time to reach the door, and then start talking," he ordered. "You tell me you want things straight once and for all. You keep saying: 'answer me' and 'keep your hands to yourself'—to make them think I'm still here. And while you're making a noise, I'll force that door."

"What happens if you run into trouble?'

"If you think there's any need, scream," Rollison said. "Jolly's within earshot—and Jolly won't take any chances."

Flo said: "Okay, but you be careful."

She pressed his hand.

"For gossake, have I been waiting for this!" Rollison said clearly, and then he stepped out of the shop entrance. He knew that the window three floors up was open, and needed no telling why. Waiting for the girl, knowing that a knife, a bullet, might strike him at any moment, had been a severe strain, but now he was on top of himself again. The door marked *Works Entrance* was not far, and he could not be seen by the men at the window. Rubbers on his boots deadened any sound he made.

He reached the door, and tried the handle. It was locked, of course, but was it bolted? There seemed no resistance at top or bottom. He used his picklock, quickly, expertly, and the lock turned. He could not believe that he would have the luck to push the door open now——

He could not; there was a bolt just above the lock. He could feel this when he pushed, but was careful not to push too hard, and make a noise which would sound above the girl's protesting voice.

He inserted another blade of the knife, but a ridge of wood overlapped, and he could not get straight at the bolt; now was the moment of testing. This blade was of high tensile steel, with a cutting edge as hard as a chisel. He levered at the wood, which was old and soft—easier than he had any right to expect. The sharp edge bit in deeper and deeper, until he was able to prise a piece off the overlap—two inches, which splintered away.

"*Stop it!*" cried Gabby's daughter, as if in alarm.

Rollison levered another piece of wood from the door and felt the chisel edge scrape the barrel of the bolt. Getting in was now only a matter of moments.

He stepped inside.

There was a pale light, high in the ceiling, showing the clock, the time-cards, the racks and the glossy walls. He went up the cement steps quickly as far as the first floor —the scene of the incidents which had made such a deep impression on him. After that he moved with extreme care, past a working floor to one where a door was marked: *Offices* and another: *Caretaker, Private*. He stood outside this for a moment, listening intently, but heard no sound. He tried the handle, fearful that it would squeak, but it did not. He pushed—but this door was locked, too.

Would it be bolted?

He took out the knife, and a tiny tin of grease, put the end of the picklock into the grease to deaden sound and lessen the risk of a scratching noise; it also made it more difficult to get a hold, and it seemed an age while he worked.

At last, the lock clicked back.

The sound was so loud that it set his heart hammering, and he stood motionless, listening for approaching footsteps. None came. He opened the door stealthily, and there was a faint squeak. He thrust it wider, and stepped inside.

Now he was in a narrow passage, leading to a kitchen and bathroom on one side, a bedroom on the other. Beyond was the living-room, with its window overlooking the street. He was aware of the sudden draught and he realized it was because the door was open. He closed it, teeth clenched with tension against the sound.

It clicked.

Rube said: "What's that?"

"What's what?" asked Parks.

"I heard something."

"You're hearing ghosts."

"I tell you I heard something!"

"There was a gust of wind," Singh said. "Came up all of a sudden."

"You go and see," Parks ordered.

There were the three of them, and they were desperate men. Rollison's one chance was to catch them by surprise. He stepped into the bathroom, left the door ajar, and saw the swarthy-faced Singh, with a throwing knife in each hand. Singh passed him. Rube came next—neck stretching out like a frightened turkey's.

"No one here," said Singh.

"I tell you I heard something!"

"Take a dekko outside," Parks ordered, and he, too, passed the bathroom.

Cautiously, Singh turned the handle of the passage door, and pulled. Now all three were near that door, and there was room for Rollison to step out, into the inner passage, and go to the front room. He had only a second, and any sound would make the others swing round and start the attack. Even with the gun, there was no guarantee that he could overcome all three.

171

He reached the doorway, back inside—then saw Singh turn his head.

"Look!" the man cried.

Rollison saw the knife raised in his hand, knew that at such a range Singh couldn't miss, darted to one side and slammed the door. He heard a knife bury itself in the wood. He snatched at the key, which was in the lock, and turned it as the men outside flung themselves against the wooden panels. The door sagged inward and he feared it would break, but the lock held. He shot the bolt, then turned to a heavy chair and pulled at it, his ribs feeling as if they must surely crack. The thudding continued and the door shook; it could not withstand this onslaught much longer. Rollison got the chair into position, gritted his teeth and pushed another behind it; he had only minutes to work in, but at least he had those minutes.

He saw the cloth-covered safe, flung the cloth back, snatched up the safe key and thrust it into the lock. It turned at the first attempt. The heavy door swung open, and Rollison saw three metal boxes. Taking one out, he carried it to the window.

Jolly, who had been round the corner, stood immediately below, holding an open sack.

Rollison dropped the first box, then hurried back for the second and third. The door sagged even farther; slowly the chairs began to move. Above the clamor Rollison heard the boxes as they clanged each against the other in the sack.

"Get going!" he called.

Jolly peered up for a moment, then turned and ran towards the motorcycle, straddled it and with the sack over his shoulder, drove off.

Gabby's daughter was now screaming: "*Police, police!*"

The police arrived as Rollison began to climb out of

the window, and before Parks and his men had the door open wide enough to get at him.

At eleven o'clock the next morning Rollison, at ease in dressing-gown and slippers, smiled at Superintendent William Grice, and pretended not to notice Perdita, behind Grice, and Jolly, behind Perdita. Grice was putting on a show of severity, but in fact he was much more relaxed than he had previously been on this affair.

"So you went to look for evidence you couldn't find?"

"I did, Bill. Sad, isn't it?"

"It was remarkable," Grice said, "but as we caught Parks and the other two with a lot of stolen goods in that flat, we aren't complaining. And I can tell you now that the man Singh was seen near Mario Bishop's place in Gill Street—we think he used a knife which he knew Syd had handled—and also near Mrs. McGuire's place in Camberwell. We found their prints at Camberwell, so we'll have all three on a charge of murder."

"Good," said Rollison. "*Very* good."

"Wonderful!" enthused Perdita.

"They say there were records of all their associates in the safe," remarked Grice.

"As a matter of fact, Bill, I think Kate McGuire probably stole those records," Rollison said airily. "She was certainly anti-Parks, that was why she was killed. But if you've got the top brass in the crimes, you don't have to worry too much about the soldiers, do you?"

"If we haven't any evidence there isn't much we can do, is there?" Grice said philosophically, "but I know one thing."

"Tell me."

"You're a very lucky man," Grice said.

"Lucky!" cried Perdita. "Why, I've never known anyone work so hard or take such risks to get results. You're lucky, you mean—you and the police force. He must be worth at least a dozen like you. And the trouble you caused him! You were as bitter as a lemon. Was it just sour grapes?"

Rollison hid a smile.

"I believed he was shielding some criminals so as to help others," Grice said. "I simply didn't believe that he hadn't been working on Osgood for a long time. I can tell you some other things, now. Parks has done all he can to implicate Osgood and clear himself. Osgood followed Kate McGuire when she took the baby away, and she shook him off near your flat. When he realized you lived near, he guessed where she had left the baby, so he came to see if Betty was here, too."

"That explains a lot," declared Perdita.

"It does indeed. And Osgood jumped to the same conclusion as I—that Kate and you had been working together for some time, Rolly, that's why he made a dead set at you. When you raided Ticky's and Kate threatened him with the scissors, he felt more sure than ever."

"I wonder why she *did* threaten him," Perdita mused.

"Poor Kate," said Rollison, sadly. "Under Osgood's thumb because of her crimes, but too frightened to tell me everything in case he found out. She risked everything for Betty and the baby, but apart from that, tried to keep a foot in both camps. If she were alive I think she would admit she told Betty to name me as the father— because if I had to defend my honor, I would save Betty from danger from Osgood."

"So you would!" cried Perdita.

"Do you know, I believe you're right," Grice said. "Well, I must be going."

Jolly saw him to the door, a few moments later. When Jolly returned, Perdita was sitting on the arm of Rollison's chair.

"Only one thing left to find out," she was saying. "Who is the father of Betty Bishop's baby."

"What *I* want to find out is how you came to handle that baby as if you were a mid-wife."

There was a pause. Then Perdita said quietly: "It's a long, long time ago, Rolly. But *my* baby died . . ." Her eyes held a far away look. Suddenly she swung round, her voice gay—over-gay, thought Jolly shrewdly, as he walked quietly from the room.

Her words followed him up the passage, and he could still hear them as he turned into the kitchen: "But I *won't* be put off. Who *is* the father?" Thoughtfully, a little sadly, he closed the door, shutting them out.

And now there was only Rollison to detect the brittleness underlying the gaiety, and only Rollison to silently applaud her courage.

He replied quietly—paying her the compliment of accepting her gaiety as such. "Next door."

Perdita looked blank.

"Once I realized that Betty herself was prepared to pretend I was the father, it was obvious," Rollison went on. "It had to be someone she loved enough to protect. Next door to her father's house in Gill Street there is a young man named Jacky Henderson . . ."

Later that evening, when the story was finished, when Perdita was saying good night, she laid a hand lightly on Rollison's arm. "Thank you," she said gently.

"Of *course* I love him," said Betty.

"Of *course* I love her," said Jacky.

"Then the quicker you're married the better," said Ma Henderson.

Syd Bishop, resplendent in a newly tailor-made suit, gave the bride away—and among the special guests were Perdita, Rollison and Jolly.

Perdita and Jolly were also guests at the baptism of Katherine Elizabeth Henderson, then three months old, when the Honorable Richard Rollison solemnly and seriously accepted the privileges and responsibilities of a godfather. More photographers and reporters appeared outside the church than had ever appeared there before —and among the waiting crowd several voices took up the chorus of a song then high in the hit parade and likely to go even higher, a song which had won the *Daily Globe* competition run by Micky Wiseman; a song called "*Hi, Pop!*"

When it was all over, Rollison took Perdita back to his flat.

"For the last time this visit," said Perdita sadly. "I'm flying to South Africa tomorrow, I feel I must go home. I didn't want you to know until the ceremony was over." After a pause she added wistfully: "Will you miss me?"

"Dreadfully."

"No, seriously."

"Very seriously."

Perdita beamed.

"That's good. Will you come and see me?"

"It depends."

"Depends on what?"

"Whether you let me carry you over my threshold again."

"You don't think I'm going to *walk*, do you?" cried Perdita.

Rollison turned the key in the lock, then swung her into his arms—the sudden ring of the telephone breaking sharply into his recollections of the first time he had carried her through this doorway. Together they ran down the passage and into the big living-room—and as Rollison picked up the receiver, Perdita took a roll of paper from her bag and pinned it to the Trophy Wall. When Rollison finished telling a newspaperman that he had nothing more to say, he looked up at the latest trophy.

It was the original score of "*Hi, Pop!*"